"Please Don't Go," Rupert Said Softly, Advancing Toward Her . . .

There was no way in the world she could avoid his compelling gaze, except by looking down, like a bashful student standing by her schoolmaster. This she was proudly determined not to do. "Miss Llanwelly," he asked her, teasingly tender, "have you any notion just how lovely you are . . . ?"

Then his mouth came down on hers. . . . His lips pressed lightly, sweetly, while he cradled her to him. Only after she had moved closer into the secure harbor of his arms and was standing on tip-toe, her mouth making a mute demand against his own, did the kiss become so all-encompassing that she was lost in a world of rapture. When he finally, ever so slowly, ever so gently, put her away from him, she was left with tightened throat, quickened breath, and quivering thighs.

"You must know how much I wanted to do that," Rupert told her in a far from steady voice, "by what I risked. . . ."

Dear Reader,

We, the editors of Tapestry Romances, are committed to bringing you two outstanding original romantic historical novels each and every month.

From Kentucky in the 1850s to the court of Louis XIII, from the deck of a pirate ship within sight of Gibraltar to a mining camp high in the Sierra Nevadas, our heroines experience life and love, romance and adventure.

Our aim is to give you the kind of historical romances that you want to read. We would enjoy hearing your thoughts about this book and all future Tapestry Romances. Please write to us at the address below.

The Editors
Tapestry Romances
POCKET BOOKS
1230 Avenue of the Americas
Box TAP
New York, N.Y. 10020

An Unforgotten Love

Jacqueline Marten

A TAPESTRY BOOK
PUBLISHED BY POCKET BOOKS NEW YORK

Books by Jacqueline Marten

English Rose
Irish Rose
French Rose
An Unforgotten Love

Published by TAPESTRY BOOKS

This novel is a work of historical fiction. Names, characters,
places and incidents relating to non-historical figures are either
the product of the author's imagination or are used fictitiously.
Any resemblance of such non-historical incidents, places or
figures to actual events or locales or persons, living or dead, is
entirely coincidental.

An *Original* publication of TAPESTRY BOOKS

A Tapestry Book published by
POCKET BOOKS, a division of Simon & Schuster, Inc.
1230 Avenue of the Americas, New York, N.Y. 10020

ISBN: 0-671-52346-5

First Tapestry Books printing April, 1985

10 9 8 7 6 5 4 3 2 1

Printed in the U.S.A.

For
my coast-to-coast nieces
and their Uncle Al . . .

Claudia Anne Isler
New York City

Heather Sutter
Milan, Pa.

Fern Laethem
Sacramento, Calif.

Judy Feinstein
Houston, Texas

ACKNOWLEDGMENT

To Miss Churchill of Enscombe

Chapter One

AT THE USUALLY UNDISTINGUISHED AGE OF fifteen, when the average English schoolgirl is both awkward and unformed, Diane Wellington-Ware had a face and figure that already gave great promise of the beauty that would be hers hereafter. She moved about Ware Place, her father's country house in Lincolnshire, with supreme confidence and grace, disdaining the advice and gentle admonitions of her governess. She scorned the clever, quiet woman who instructed her as only the proud and pretty can despise the plain and dull.

Grief may come to those of any appearance,

1

but there was no doubt that when Diane attended the memorial service for both her parents, the ethereal loveliness of her small pale face earned her an added tithe of public compassion. Murmurs of sympathy broke out as she walked down the church aisle, head held high, her great gray-blue eyes lustrous with tears, golden curls covered only by a sheer black chiffon veil hanging loose over the shoulders and back of her exquisitely expensive mourning dress.

Instinctively she responded to the murmurs and to the moment's respectful hush that followed, kneeling briefly in the pew, then taking her seat, hands clasped, head reverently bent.

In truth, though she was sorry, of course, that her parents were dead, Diane's suffering was minimal. She had not been too well acquainted with Sir Reginald and Lady Wellington-Ware—for they had led a very busy social life in London —but on their infrequent trips to Lincolnshire they had petted and praised and spoiled her extravagantly. She was more frequently than usual excused from the schoolroom and her music practice.

Still, they had not played an important role in her life and had perished in a most typical way when their friend Lord Hatton's yacht sank off the coast of Spain. Even in Lincolnshire, gossip had leaked back of her mother's connection with Lord Hatton as well as her father's closeness to Lady Charlotte Hatton.

Bored by the minister's tribute to the goodness and piety of her parents, Diane's wandering mind dwelled briefly on the odd relationships of the Hattons and the Wellington-Wares.

I daresay, she decided matter-of-factly, *that they'll get it all sorted out in heaven.*

That the adulterous four could be anywhere but in heaven never occurred to Diane, for Victoria would not mount the throne for another eight years, and the Hattons were rich and titled while the Wellington-Wares were *her* parents. Miss Diane was comfortably aware that God granted favors to the higher ranks that lesser mortals could not expect.

She had no worries for her own future. As long as she could remember she had lived at Ware Place in the particular charge of her much older half brother, now Sir William, and his wife Mary, whose many pregnancies had never produced a living baby.

Diane was their substitute child, and she would be doubly so now, she reflected complacently an hour or two later as she flitted about the drawing room of their home, receiving the condolences of friends and family with eyes full of soulful sorrow and lips that contrived to quiver without any special effort.

Her first act as a full daughter to Sir William and his plump Mary was to induce them to dismiss her governess and secure one who was more "sympathetic," by which she meant one who did not place such stress on the reading of literature, knowledge of the history of her country and a familiarity with figures that would enable her one day to do household accounts.

"As though," Diane told her maid, shaking her golden curls triumphantly the day the governess was banished, "I have need of such information. What else are servants for?"

She managed to be present when new candidates for the position of her mentor had their interviews. The first had been recommended by the vicar.

"She's much too pert," Diane told her sister-in-law in an audible aside. What she meant was that the auburn-haired young lady being examined was far too pretty and unafraid.

The second applicant had been sent by Mrs. Bulwark, Lady Mary Wellington-Ware's close friend. Miss Simmons was past thirty, with no pretensions to good looks, but she had a quiet air of self-possession and such piercing dark eyes, Diane had the uncomfortable notion they could see right through her, a state of affairs not to be endured.

"She's ugly, Mary; I really couldn't abide having her about me all the time."

Sweet, simple Lady Wellington-Ware hastened to dismiss her dear friend's choice.

The third candidate, Miss Ettington, had advertised herself in the *Times*. She was shabby and to Diane seemed middle-aged, not disagreeable to look at but sadly nearsighted and painfully anxious to please. She had never been a private governess before, but worked in a day school the past eight years so she could take care of an ailing father in the evenings. When he died—quite recently—his pension died with him and his house had been willed to an only son.

She'll do, decided Diane, with a nod of approval toward Mary.

Miss Ettington needed the position desperately, that was clear, so Miss Diane Wellington-Ware would rule *her*, not the other way round. Diane would be able to learn *what* she wanted *when* she wanted, and there would be no complaints from her, thought the pupil, smiling with great sweetness at the governess, about lack of respect or fuss if one got just a little cross and happened to toss a book.

Miss Ettington, whose nearsighted eyes saw more than she was given credit for, knew only too well what was in store for her, but she was determined to endure. For the sake of an attic room furnished with cast-offs from the rest of the house, three sustaining meals a day grudgingly brought to her on a tray by the upstairs maid and twenty-five pounds a year—which might later increase to thirty if she gave satisfaction—she was determined to endure.

Endure she did for a full two years, a long two years, occasionally managing to stuff a few facts into Miss Diane's reluctant head but more often serving as a lady-in-waiting to that imperious young beauty.

At just past seventeen, Miss Diane saw no

need to continue learning. She was breathtakingly beautiful, the belle of the local balls. She had the wardrobe of a princess and a natural skill at flirtation that required no coaching. She could play three popular waltzes on the spinet with dash and verve and accompany herself while she sang "The Last Rose Of Summer" in a voice of melting tenderness. Her needlepoint chair cover (finished by Lady Wellington-Ware) could be pointed out in the dining room, and the parlor walls were hung with her painted flowers.

What more could a young man want and what need for a young lady to be constrained any longer by a governess?

She sought an interview with Sir William and his lady to state her case. Fondly and foolishly, they agreed with her. Miss Ettington received her month's notice and, armed with a fulsome reference, posted off to a new position with Mrs. Bulwark's niece in Derbyshire.

Shortly before her nineteenth birthday Diane Wellington-Ware had her coming out in London, and during her first season Sir William received and—at his sister's behest—refused three gratifying requests for her hand in marriage.

Sir Thomas Ludlum's lineage was impeccable, true, but his estate was small and he preferred to spend most of the year in Yorkshire. Yorkshire, ugh! shuddered Diane after due consideration. One might as well be exiled to the colonies.

Commander Leakey was rich, to be sure, but really not rich enough to overcome her aversion to his rough red complexion, his booming voice and, most of all, that name. She could not—no, really she could not be expected to go through life as Diane Leakey!

Lord Fortescue had wealth, great estates, above all, the title she coveted; but balanced against these were his age and appearance. He was in his mid-fifties and wrinkled as a monkey, yet for all that, there was something spry and healthy about him. Those short skinny men had a habit of going on forever. If she married him, she might be *my lady*, but with a good ten or twenty years of waiting to be a widow.

She would do better in her second season.

Her besotted guardians agreed and carried her off to Lincolnshire to rest and recruit her strength for the next winter's mating rites.

When the season came round, the proposals poured in, but none were acceptable. Most of her offers, unfortunately, came from men with an eye to Sir William's fortune and who proffered little in return.

During her third season, to her brother's consternation, as well as her own, Diane Wellington-Ware fell madly in love with Lieutenant Harlan Page, who had nothing to recommend him but the body of a Greek god and an incredibly handsome face.

His hair was as golden as her own but curled

short all about his head and face. His eyes were an even deeper blue than hers and seemed perpetually dancing with merriment. His nose and cheekbones, chin and forehead seemed to have been chiseled from pink marble by an artist rather than created by nature, they were such marvels of perfect masculine beauty.

He had little money, no family, a doubtful future in the army. There was no benefit in wanting him or wedding him, yet she was carried away by the wanting and stubbornly determined on the wedding. With the obstinacy of a nature that had never known denial, she who had said nay to a baronet, a rich naval officer and a viscount bent all her efforts to attaching an impecunious army lieutenant who offered only good looks, good humor and a warm heart.

Not given to reflection or to self-examination, Diane could not know that the first love of her life was herself. Lieutenant Harlan Page, in a male version, was the very image of Diane Wellington-Ware. Loving him was another form of self-love.

The securing of Lieutenant Page's affections was easily achieved. The consent of her guardian was not. Sir William and his lady opposed the degrading match with unexpected vigor. Diane laughed at their dismay and defied them. They threatened to throw her off if she persisted in her folly. She smiled and disbelieved them.

In view of the past, she might be pardoned for reasoning that, once the union was an accomplished fact, they would come round. Had they not always?

She waited the necessary few months until she was of age, and her guardians could not legally prevent her. Held in the house of Harlan Page's colonel, her wedding was attended only by his fellow officers, with a scattering of their wives.

On her bridegroom's arm, Diane returned to Ware House on Wimpole Street, laughingly prepared to forgive and be lovingly forgiven. William and Mary were not at home. The hallway was heaped with trunks and boxes and bags containing her clothes and personal possessions.

Diane selected one trunk to take with her and told Dawkins, the butler, "Inform Sir William and Lady Wellington-Ware that I will send for the rest in a fortnight when I return from my honeymoon."

She was their adored sister–daughter. In a fortnight, she was confidently sure, they would welcome her with open arms. Open hearts. Most important, open purses.

Not the slightest doubt of it shadowed her honeymoon in Brighton or interfered with two weeks of unalloyed felicity.

Harlan was so adorable and so adoring. Everywhere they went, girls and women, even old ladies, stared at him in wide-eyed admiration and at her in awed envy.

The new Mrs. Harlan Page was fully aware of what a breathtakingly beautiful couple she and her lieutenant made and found not a little part of Harlan's charm in his complete unawareness of his own incredible good looks.

It was doubly delightful to Diane to be loved so passionately and to have a husband so humbly grateful to *her* for loving *him*.

He came to her bed each night and wooed her with tender gentle ardor until after a week she succumbed and allowed him to complete his lovemaking. Their second week they spent more time in their bedchamber than walking on the Parade. Once she discovered the pleasure of sexual gratification, she became so insatiably eager to satisfy this new desire the exhaustedly happy Harlan could scarce be blamed for believing he had discovered earthly paradise.

On the newlywed couple's return from Brighton, Diane over ruled her husband's quiet suggestion that they stop first at their lodgings. Instead they proceeded at once to Wimpole Street. She could scarcely wait to tell William and Mary how felicitous her marriage was and how right she had been.

Sir William and Lady Wellington-Ware, the butler informed her as snubbingly as the out-of-favor beauty had used to speak to him, had departed for Lincolnshire a se'nnight before.

"But my clothing!" Diane said indignantly, looking about the hallway as though she expected her trunks and bags still to be sitting there after two weeks.

"I have been h-instructed," said Dawkins—in

the intensity of his pleasure reverting to his cockney origins—"that, should you call, you were to be told to h-address h-any h-inquiries to Sir William's solicitor, Mr. Frederick Saxon."

Diane shot Dawkins a look of furious loathing, then turned on her heel to leave, dragging on her husband's arm as he paused for a murmured "Thank you" to the butler.

In the carriage the new Mrs. Page wept the angry frustrated tears of a spoiled child. "How could they leave me like this?" she wailed to her husband with characteristic disregard for the facts.

He soothed and petted her as she was accustomed to be soothed and petted, so that by the time they had left off their luggage and were on their way to see the attorney, her natural buoyancy had been completely restored.

William and Mary were trying to punish her a little, which was rather unkind of them, to be sure, but the type of spitefulness Diane could understand and almost be in charity with.

She sat smiling, thinking of their journey into Lincolnshire a few weeks hence . . . her brother's joy to receive her back and Mary's happy tears. Then the reception that would be held in honor of her marriage at Ware Place to make up for the shabbiness of her wedding. As a new bride Mary would surely lend her the Wellington-Ware diamond necklace and tiara.

In all of her glowing visions, Harlan, though he still wore his dashing regimentals, was no longer in the army but had become a permanent fixture at Ware Place.

Mr. Frederick Saxon soon scattered these roseate dreams. In a voice as dry and dusty as the leather bindings of the law books stacked behind him, he informed Mrs. Harlan Page that the Wellington-Wares wanted no part of her.

All her clothing and personal goods had been stored in a warehouse, which, he added prosaically, was paid up to the end of the month. He reached into a drawer and extended a slip of paper. "Here is the receipt."

Diane sat motionless, seemingly turned to stone, so her husband accepted the receipt and folded it into his tunic pocket.

"B-but they can't d-do this to m-me," Diane stammered presently. "They *love* me. I'm like their daughter."

"As to that . . ." The lawyer formed a tent with his pressed fingertips and studied them with great interest. "Sir William has formed the intention of adopting a nephew of Lady Wellington-Ware's—I believe, her brother's third son."

"You can't mean *Spotty Scotty!*" Diane cried out incredulously.

"The young man's name is Scott Banning," Mr. Saxon told her reprovingly, "but it is proposed—and his family is willing—that he take the Wellington-Ware name so that it will not die out with Sir William."

"But what about *me?*" Diane's voice rose to a

near scream. "Did not my father leave anything to me?"

"All your father's property and money went to Sir William, as well as his own mother's fortune, which was considerably more. There was no entail on the property, no restricting prohibitions. It is his to dispose of as he wishes."

Diane was trembling with shock. Even as her husband murmured, "I can take care of you, darling," she was demanding, "Am I to have nothing?"

"Your mother's settlement was to be given you on your marriage. I have administered it for Sir William these last few years, and he most generously did not draw on it for your keep or expenses, as he was legally entitled to do. It, therefore, comes to you intact."

"How much?"

"In the neighborhood of twelve thousand pounds. I have the figures right here."

He took a sheet from a file on his desk and handed it across to Lieutenant Page, but Diane intercepted it. She scanned the sheet for a few minutes, then tossed it onto the desk in disgust. None of her governesses had succeeded in making her understand a column of figures; Miss Ettington had not even tried.

"I don't understand it," she said petulantly.

Mr. Saxon lifted the page. "Twelve thousand two hundred and twenty-nine pounds, nine shillings and eight pence," he recited precisely. "Prudently invested—I suggest, just as it is now—it should bring you in an income of six to seven hundred a year."

"There, darling, isn't that wonderful news?" Harlan murmured encouragingly to his bride.

"Well, it's better than nothing," she conceded ungraciously, then turned again to Mr. Saxon. "When can I have it all made over to me?"

"Whenever you wish, the whole can be made over to your husband."

"My husband! But it's *my* money!"

"Surely you are aware that under the law, my dear Mrs. Page, a husband controls his wife's money."

Before Diane could explode in indignation, Harlan broke in soothingly, "I married my wife for love, Mr. Saxon. I neither need nor desire her money. I have my pay and a small income from my father's estate to support her. Let her own money come to her for dress and personal expenses. I will sign whatever papers are necessary."

"My dear sir, however generous and disinterested, I must strongly suggest—"

"Lieutenant Page has told you what he wishes," Diane interrupted, with a fond and glowing look at her obliging husband as she ran her gloved fingertips up and down his arm. "Be so kind as to draw up the papers he spoke of directly."

"If you still wish me to act for you," Mr. Saxon said with no great enthusiasm.

Diane shrugged. "I suppose you'll do as well as any other."

Mr. Saxon took several deep controlled breaths, reminding himself that Sir William, like his father before him, was an old and valued client. For their sakes, he would do his reluctant best for the beautiful little bitch that the one had sired and the other had so understandably disowned.

Chapter Two

IT WAS EARLY AFTERNOON WHEN HARLAN PAGE, in all the glory of his month-old captain's uniform, his hat carried correctly under his arm, entered his wife's bedroom.

Diane sat in the middle of the big fourposter while her maid Amy, bent over at an awkward angle, brushed out her golden curls. The river of tears that ran down the beauty's face did not rob her skin of radiance; weeping appeared to enhance rather than dim the luminous loveliness of her eyes.

"My darling," cried the captain in genuine distress, "whatever is wrong?"

He sat down on the edge of the bed and reached over to her. By the time she was comfortably nestled in his strong arms, Amy had melted discreetly away, with only one exasperated look heavenward to convey her feelings to a hovering footman in the hallway.

Left alone with him in the bedroom, the captain's wife sniffed woefully. "Everything's wrong. I was most dreadfully sick all morning, and you left without telling me, and I have *such* a headache, and Cook was impertinent when I complained about last night's dinner. I really think we should dismiss her . . . I heard about a wonderful French chef last week at Lady Salisbury's party . . ."

She peeped up and saw the frown beginning to crease Harlan's dear handsome face. She could see his lips begin to move and fancied the words being formed were *We can't afford.* . . .

Before he could actually say them, she began sobbing with renewed vigor. "My new blue and gold evening gown is already too tight around the waist. I'm getting f-fat and ugly, and you won't l-love m-me anym-more."

What could an adoring husband do but smooth her headache away with his own two hands, remind her that he had been on guard duty this morning and had left quickly and quietly so as not to waken her, and renew his daily assurance that her morning sickness never lasted above a few minutes? Most of all, to reiterate again and again, that she was the most beautiful woman in England and he would love her till the end of time.

Encouraged by her smiles and cooing sounds of pleasure, Harlan ventured next to suggest that the clever new seamstress she had found—Mrs. Acres, wasn't that her name?—could surely let out her dress so that it could be worn for another party or two.

Diane, who had already told Mrs. Acres to alter her gown, snuggled deeper into her husband's embrace, and he kissed the soft hand that was nearest to his lips.

"And will you take care of Cook?" she whispered presently.

"Let me speak to her. She deserves at least another chance."

"Of course, dearest. Whatever you say. It was *your* colonel she served such a poor dinner to. I was positively ashamed, but you are always so patient and forbearing, my love."

"I did notice," said Harlan slowly as she turned in bed so he could unfasten a row of little cloth-covered buttons at the back of her nightrobe, "that the mutton was sadly underdone."

Since he could not see her face, Diane made no attempt to repress the triumphant smile curving her lips. "And the barley soup," she mentioned casually. "Why, I read somewhere that Count—Count what's-his-name—you know, the eccentric one who studied nourishment for

18

the poor—recommended it for them, but I blushed to see it at *our* table."

"I will indeed speak to Cook," Harlan repeated a great deal more decisively than before, and Diane was content to let the matter rest. In just a short time, she felt certain, Cook would be dismissed and she would have her French chef.

Unexpectedly, Diane proved to be out in her calculations. A man whose regiment is ordered off to India and expects his wife to follow him as soon as possible, has no need of such refinements as English cooks *or* French chefs.

"India!" cried Diane, fear for once distorting her pretty features. "You can't go to that barbarous place and leave me. I'm pregnant!"

"You will be coming there, too, my darling."

"Are you mad, Harlan? The journey takes months, and I expect to be brought to bed in less than two. Are you suggesting I have a baby on shipboard like a slave from Africa or some slut on her way to Australia?"

"No, no, darling, you shall stay in England until the baby is born, with some competent woman to take care of you until you can both come out to India. Perhaps some sergeant's wife who would be glad to have her journey out paid—most of them cannot go otherwise."

"But *you* won't be with me when I need you," Diane told him pathetically.

"You will have the doctor and the midwife and your maid Amy, as well as the companion we hire," he tried to cheer her. "Before I leave, I will arrange it all, so you will be well looked after; it will give me time out there to look around and secure a villa for us. I shall—"

"A villa?" Diane interrupted, brightening. The word had a grand ring to it.

"Oh, yes, a beautiful villa, with gardens and terraces and balconies. *And* servants. We will be able to afford dozens of servants in India, you know. And I hear the social life is very gay, while business opportunities abound. Many a man has quit the military there to make his private fortune."

"Oh, Harlan, that would be wonderful!" She clasped her hands ecstatically. "What fun if we were to be rich, far richer even than William and Mary. If you were to become a baronet one day and *I* were to be *My Lady*. Oh, how I would like to throw that in their faces!"

"I will try to give you everything your heart desires!" promised the bewitched husband, kneeling at her feet in effect if not in fact.

"Oh Harlan, I do love you!" she sighed in return, and innocently, they both believed it to be true.

Her situation was less happy after Harlan left with his regiment. Most of her friends were among the military, and only a handful were now left in London, their numbers even further reduced by the end of the spring social season and the beginning of warm weather. All those who could afford to do so or who received invitations from friends or family fled to the country or the seaside.

Diane had no such invitations but, in any event, was constrained to stay in London in easy reach of her physician. Jeannie MacFarlane, the sergeant's wife hired for her by Harlan, was a sturdy sensible soul. Diane accepted her hard work but turned up her straight, proud Wellington-Ware nose at having her for a companion. What had she in common with a Jeannie Mac-Farlane?

As for Jeannie . . . "I'd sooner scrub the floors from cellar to roof than spend a half hour in her ladyship's company," she sniffed to Diane's maid. "Fair tiring it is, so full of havers she is."

"You don't know the half of it," sniffed Amy. "At least the mistress never threw her hairbrush or perfume bottle at *you*."

"No, and she never better had, if she wants to keep her health!" Jeannie retorted. "How you stand it, lass."

Amy shrugged. "The pay is fairer than some, and the food's good. It's not as though the likes of you and I can pick and choose."

All the differences in station and viewpoint melted away on the night when Diane's pains began. Then they were just three women together.

The footman was dispatched for the doctor and midwife, and while they waited Jeannie and Amy cleaned up Diane's bed and then her person. She was put into a fresh cotton nightdress and the glorious golden hair made into two thick braids. They tied knotted towels to the bedpost for her to tug at, held her down gently when she would have thrown herself off the bed and kept applying cool cloths to her heated face and forehead.

And through it all, they offered encouragement—Amy's kindly, Jeannie's bracing—when she screamed as much with terror as with the agony of the birth pangs.

When the physician arrived with his midwife attendant, Diane would not allow the maid and the sergeant's wife to be sent away. She clung to them fiercely, the only friendly faces in an unfamiliar world of cruelty and pain.

Toward the end of her labor, she cursed her husband with long-forgotten words culled from the recesses of her memory from her times in Sir Reginald's stables. "I hate him! I hate him!" she shrieked when she had breath enough to speak. "How could he do this to me?"

Her labor went on all through the night and into the next day.

On June 28, 1838, midway through the coronation of Queen Victoria, Diane Wellington-Ware Page gave a final thrust and heave and a blood-curdling scream, and Diane Victoria Page, yelling her own displeasure, slid into the doctor's waiting hands.

Chapter Three

"I DON'T UNDERSTAND, MR. SAXON," DIANE SAID petulantly, averting her eyes from the account book that he had pushed across his desk for her inspection. "You know I have no head for figures."

The solicitor sighed gustily. He did indeed know that.

"It is quite simple, Mrs. Page, if you will only apply yourself. During the years before your husband went to India, the two of you barely lived within your income, even though, in addition to your own money, you had his army pay, some money I gather he made from gambling and the interest on the legacy from his father, which is now tied up in your daughter and cannot be touched."

A spasm of irritation crossed his face at the blank look on hers.

"In the four years since his death," he continued testily, "your spending has far outpaced your income, and you have eaten steadily into your capital. When you disburse your capital, you have a temporary increase of cash on hand, but in the long run, you suffer. With less capital, you have less income, and if you keep on in the way you have been going," he wound up with a sudden burst of outraged emotion, "in another two or three years you will be penniless and forced to earn your bread!"

Diane stared at him in dazed disbelief. "Earn my bread!" she echoed with a kind of horrified fascination.

"Earn your bread," he repeated with grim relish. Then his tone altered. He said almost sadly, "I have written to Sir William of your difficulties . . . I regret . . ." A helpless little gesture completed the sentence.

"I hope you told William that *I* did not ask for his help!" said the widowed Mrs. Page with the same imperious tilt to her chin as Miss Wellington-Ware of Ware Place.

"Pride is all very well, Mrs. Page," Mr. Saxon admonished her, not without the first faint glimmer of admiration he had ever felt toward her, "but it doesn't take the place of money."

"What must I do?" asked Diane.

"Retrench in your expenses. Vigorously—and at once. Your house must be given up. It is much too large and uneconomical. You have far too many servants eating off their heads at your expense. Give up your parties. *And* dressmakers. *And* rich foods and wines."

"You are telling me what I must not allow myself," Diane said bitterly. "What may I have?"

"My advice—other than marrying again, which I must confess I long ago expected you to do or we would have had this conversation far sooner—is to take a cottage away from London with just a couple of sturdy country maids to serve all your needs. Living in this modest way, your income should completely cover your expenses and permit you to educate your daughter as Sir Reginald's granddaughter should be. Her other grandfather's legacy will provide her with a modest dowry."

"I had not thought of marrying again," Diane murmured.

"It seems the natural—er—solution for a—woman of your—er—youth and beauty." He coughed a little. "You have no—no prospects?" he inquired delicately.

Diane applied a lace-edged handkerchief to dewy eyes. "You see, after my husband . . . ."

It was true that the first extravagance of her grief for Harlan had been wild and prolonged, and mingled with it—though, guiltily, she never allowed this to the forefront of her mind—was a deep and burning anger at him for deserting her so selfishly, dying quickly and ingloriously of a fever only six weeks after he reached India, shattering all their hopes and dreams.

After the first year, however, when she could lay aside her mourning, she had discovered that to be a young, beautiful widow—pitied, admired, talked about—suited her admirably.

Partying, dining and dancing were the breath of life to her; the art of celibate flirtation brought its own exquisite pleasure. A few moonlight kisses and, when her gown was especially low cut, occasionally a little groping in some darkened antechamber of a ballroom both stimulated and satisfied her senses. The former ecstacy of passion had been blotted out, never to return, by the remembered twin horrors of pregnancy and birth.

Mr. Saxon was rapidly leafing through the papers in her file box, embarrassed by the atmosphere of emotion. He paused at one sheet. "Hmm," he said aloud, then as Diane looked at him in plaintive inquiry, "I have here"—he tapped the sheet—"a possible solution to your problem. The house at St. Ives, the one where your husband's father spent his last years after his own retirement from the navy—it's part of your daughter's legacy. It has been let to a number of tenants over the past ten years but has been standing empty the last seven or eight months. A foolish waste. This might be the very home for you. No purchase or rent and a low upkeep, which is being charged against the estate even while it is vacant."

"Where is St. Ives?" Diane asked.

"In Cornwall. A lovely seaport town. The house, I understand, stands on a high cliff overlooking the sea."

"Let me consider a few days," Diane told him softly, even while every fiber of her being rejected the notion. Cornwall! The end of nowhere! If she must take a husband—and that was the one part of Mr. Saxon's advice she had taken to heart—then Cornwall was not the place to seek him out. London. In London alone would she find the right kind of man to suit her . . .

But not encumbered by financial problems and a daughter. Men were enticed by beautiful widows but not by the child of another man!

If only she were free to set herself up in an elegant set of apartments needing only a personal maid. She could easily keep up her standards then.

Walking along the streets after she left the solicitor's offices, she nibbled distractedly at the middle finger of one glove, so preoccupied with her thoughts, she wandered aimlessly, not conscious of where she was heading.

The smells gradually brought Diane to greater awareness, and she looked around with shock at the narrow, noxious street where she had gotten to, full of women with painted faces and rough-looking men who eyed her with a mixture of cupidity and contempt.

She looked about desperately for a carriage, and failing that, someone to give her directions. A shabby–genteel-looking woman came toward her, a basket over her arm. She stared hard at Diane, then turned about abruptly, retracing her steps.

Diane hurried after her, unwilling to lose the only person she had seen in the last few minutes who did not vaguely frighten her.

"Miss. Ma'am. I seem to have lost my way. Would you accompany me to the nearest place where I can hire a hackney? I will gladly pay you." She fumbled at the strings of her purse. "Shall we say, a shilling?"

"You need not pay me," the woman said with dignity. "It is just two or three streets away. Come." And then, as Diane seemed intent on extracting the shilling from her purse, she cautioned sharply, "Don't show your money here."

Diane looked at her companion as they marched side by side together. "I know you, I think," she said in a puzzled way.

A sad tired face was turned all the way toward her. "Yes, Miss Diane, you do," said a quiet composed voice.

"Why—" Diane gasped. "You're Miss Ettington."

"Yes, Miss Diane," said the same weary voice, "I am."

"Mrs. Page," Diane corrected automatically. "But I thought you went to Mrs. Bulwark's niece, Mrs. . . . Mrs. . . ."

"Mrs. Blakely," Miss Ettington supplied. "But that's ancient history. After I was no longer needed there, I was employed by the Southeys, then finally the Worthingtons. Unfortunately, Mr. Worthington thought the duties of any female who served in his house included personal services to him. One evening while he was trying to induce me to agree, his wife came upon us. Naturally, I was the one dismissed without a reference *or* my last quarter's pay."

Probably the other way around, Diane decided cruelly. As though any man would go out of his way for such a dull, drab-looking creature. Not— she shrugged mentally—that she blamed Miss Ettington for trying to advance her interests. In this world a woman had to do what she could for herself however she could. Wasn't she, Diane Page, even now planning to do the same? But, wisely, with marriage lines and a fortune to protect her? And, of course, her own special beauty and elegance for bait.

She nibbled at her glove again. If only she could make the money last . . . if only she could get out from under her burdens. . . .

And then an incredible and wonderful thought struck her. Surely fate had brought the two of them together here this day. Cautiously she made her first move, inquiring without too great eagerness, "Have you a position now, Miss Ettington?"

"Certainly." Ironically. "I work at the Sign of the Three Feathers two blocks from here—as a barmaid."

"A barmaid!" Diane was genuinely shocked. "But you're a gentlewoman!"

"A gentlewoman who likes to eat, Miss Diane."

"Mrs. Page," she corrected again. "I'm a widow."

"My condolences."

"It's been four years. Miss Ettington,"—she had made up her mind—"would you like to live in a fine home in Cornwall by the sea and take care of the house and a four-year-old girl? You could have a local woman in—oh, say once a week to do the heavy work, but otherwise you would be responsible for everything. The buying and housekeeping and the meals. I could only give you a salary of—er—twenty pounds a year and expenses," she continued rapidly, having calculated the smallest amount she could get away with, "but you would have a lovely home . . . you would really be the mistress there," she babbled on.

"Is something wrong with the child? Is she simpleminded?"

"Of course not," Diane denied indignantly.

"Vicky is an exceptionally clever, talented, interesting child," she went on with no idea that she was stating the truth, for the daily half-hour regulation tea-time visit of mother and daughter had given Diane no greater acquaintance with her daughter than her parents had shared with her.

"Vicky?"

"Diane Victoria, my daughter."

"You will not be coming to Cornwall with us?"

"No." Diane brushed nervously at her skirt. "I have commitments here in town, but I have to think of Vicky. The air of London is so bad; our doctor thinks she needs a more salubrious climate. And, of course, I could *never* send her away with someone untrustworthy . . . or not well-bred. I would expect you to—"

"There is a hackney." Miss Ettington lifted the arm that held her basket and waved it with great animation. "I accept your offer," she told Diane baldly, opening the carriage door.

"How soon can you come to me?"

"This instant."

"Don't you have to collect your things? Give notice?"

"I have nothing worthwhile to collect," Miss Ettington said cheerfully. "Nothing is safe in the room I rent, so everything I value I carry with me." She tapped her basket. "As for the work . . ." She shrugged. "When I don't turn up, Tim will hire someone else."

"Follow me then," said Diane almost gayly and stepped up into the carriage.

"I think—after this—you are bound to appreciate Cornwall," she said condescendingly when Miss Ettington was seated beside her.

"Pray tell me more about my pupil," countered Miss Ettington, a governess once again.

Chapter Four

Miss Ettington knelt in the small garden that she had lovingly and laboriously nourished during her three years at Cliff House in Cornwall.

"That which we call a rose, by any other name would smell as sweet," she said aloud, a fingertip moving gently over one of the closed buds. "Oh, I do think Shakespeare is wrong about that, don't you?" she addressed the rose. "It just wouldn't be the same, would it, my beauty, if you were called a dandelion?"

"Now there's a question will occupy my mind many a night now," said a deep amused voice behind her. "And to think I never even thought of it before."

Miss Ettington scrambled to her feet, her cheeks more scarlet than the roses. To the brawny, brown-faced man standing there in his patched trousers and flannel shirt, with a knitted fisherman's cap in his hand, she looked adorably confused and lovely, never mind the lines on her face, the gray streaks in her dark hair, the earth-dirty work-roughened hands.

"Mr. Llanwelly, how you startled me!" She ignored his comment and her own embarrassment. "Was there something that you wanted, sir?" she asked, pitching her voice primly high.

"Miss Vicky was down at the shore today when I brought my boat in." He smiled teasingly. "She said it was *you* who had need of *me*, Miss Ettington, ma'am."

Her blush deepened. "I—yes, well I—the fence for the goat—he keeps breaking out. And there's a leak in the roof over the stall for Vicky's pony. If you could get to one or both today . . ."

"I'll not leave tonight till everything is ship-shape, ma'am."

"I thank you, Mr. Llanwelly."

"You should know by now you don't have to thank me for being of service to you," he told her with great simplicity. "It's my pleasure, ma'am, besides which," he added quite naturally, "the extra coin comes in handy. There aren't enough fish in the sea to stock the cupboard for those

34

three hungry boys of mine or keep Sunday shoes on their feet."

"Nevertheless, sir, I am obliged to you for coming so speedily."

"Egan," he told her. "I keep telling you, my name is Egan, not Mr. Llanwelly or sir."

"So you keep telling me, *Egan*," she retorted with bitter emphasis, "and all the while you *miss* and ma'am *me*. I question that you even know what my name is."

He took one step nearer to her, and the rumble of his voice was like a rough caress. "You've a name as sweet as your roses, Miss Caroline Ettington, but we both know, lass, I may not use it. You're the lady of Cliff House with Miss Vicky in your charge, and I'm just another fisherman from the row of shanties near the shore. My Annie—God rest her—was born to the life, but even if I would consider—could you give up Miss Vicky?"

He saw terror leap out of her eyes at the very notion. All the color had fled the glowing cheeks. "No!" she cried. "Of course not!" She crossed her arms against her breast, as though by that primitive gesture, she could hold back the secret fear deep within her, the only real fear she had known in these last years . . . that one day Diane Wellington-Ware Page would appear, an accepted suitor in tow, perhaps even a husband, and wrest Vicky out of her keeping. Her beloved Vicky, her heart's daughter, so much dearer to

Caroline Ettington than she would ever be to her own mother.

At supper that evening, which it had become their custom to take in the kitchen except on Sundays when they practiced propriety by using the small dining parlor, Vicky put down the sketching pad that was never far from her hand. There was a troubled frown on her face. "Is mama coming to visit, Aunt Etti?" she asked.

Miss Ettington's hand trembled so, the tea from her cup slopped over into the saucer. "Not that I have heard, Vicky," she tried to say casually, even as the same dread fear hollowed out her insides. "Why do you ask?"

"You've gone away from me," Vicky pointed out. "You only go away from me like that when mama comes to visit," she added with the matter-of-fact wisdom that made her seem so much older than seven.

Seeing Miss Ettington's stricken face, the child jumped up from her chair and stumbled gladly into the arms held out to her. The governess stroked the soft hair, so much less golden and abundant than her mother's, smiled into blue eyes that could not compare in brilliance with the older Diane's but more than made up for this lack by their bright intelligence.

"I shall never go away from you, my Vicky," she pledged softly, even as she prayed it was a promise she would never have to break.

It was foolish of her to worry so, she told herself that night in her bedroom long after

Vicky was asleep in hers. Mrs. Page had not visited her daughter for seven—no, it was nearer to eight months now.

Their first year in Cornwall she had come faithfully four times, descending on them in a cloud of expensive perfume and silk, fine lawn or velvet—whatever was appropriate to the season. She had approved all Miss Ettington's arrangements, seemed pleased by Vicky's earlier joyous welcomes, but been barely able to control her impatience to be away again.

At each coming Miss Ettington had braced herself for the words that would spell an end to this heavenly new life, and every time Diane Page had made it clear there would be no change. Her own new life, unburdened by child, was more than heavenly, too.

The second year she had only visited twice, so that in between the two times, it was pleasant and easy to forget her. Just so long as the money came. . . . There had been that one period when Diane went abroad and quite forgot to send the quarterly payment. Miss Ettington had had to use up her own scant savings and get in debt to the local storekeepers until her employer returned to England and found the governess's frantic letters reminding her of her obligations.

After that the arrangement had been improved. The payments came direct from a solicitor's office, and Miss Ettington breathed easier, except that now and then a word, a thought brought back the old nightmare fear. Diane might not want the child, but that was no guarantee that Vicky would be hers forever.

Almost as though her own fears had conjured up the evil, a letter came from London a few days later. Over the imperiously scrawled *Diane W-W Page* was a single terse direction: Prepare the best bedroom. The real mistress of Cliff House would be arriving soon—no specific date given—to spend a few weeks.

A few weeks! Miss Ettington's heart plunged to the level of her stout gardening boots. Never before had Mrs. Page stayed so long with them. On the other hand—her heart soared up again—if she were planning to take Vicky away with her, she would hardly pay a long visit.

Miss Ettington's mind went round and round in unhappy circles, even as she moved Vicky from the large best bedroom at the front of the house into her own more modestly sized room overlooking the sea. A connecting door from it led through to a third small bedroom, but cannily Miss Ettington did not make use of it. By moving herself up to the one huge attic room, the fictional status of her position would be preserved. If Diane and her daughter were on the second floor, it was only fitting for the governess to be isolated in the attic.

Told of the impending visit, as well as the new arrangements, Vicky gave a solemn little nod. "Don't worry, Aunt Etti," she said comfortingly. "We will be happy again when she is gone."

"Vicky!" Miss Ettington was genuinely shocked

"She's your mother. You—you—" She looked into the bright blue eyes staring at her so inquiringly. "You really mustn't talk about her like that," she finished lamely.

"Why not?" asked Vicky in genuine curiosity. "We aren't happy when she comes, are we?"

"Oh, Vicky!"

"At least *I'm* not so very happy," Vicky specified scrupulously. "And I don't think"—the wise little monkey-look that almost frightened Miss Ettington was back on her nut-brown face—"I don't think you are," she added, peering up at Aunt Etti's flushed face.

Miss Ettington opened her mouth to make a pious observation about mothers and daughters and then abruptly pressed her lips tight shut again. She simply would not play the hypocrite with this beloved child.

After Vicky danced off to bring her pencils and crayons and drawing paraphernalia from her usual bedroom to her temporary one, her mentor laughed aloud ruefully. Just as well she had kept her tongue between her teeth. The beloved *and* precocious child would not have believed her anyhow.

Her daughter's thoughts could not hurt Diane, but hypocrisy from the one she loved most— Miss Ettington's heart swelled up in happiness that it should be she—could certainly hurt Diane's ruthlessly straightforward daughter!

Two days later a carriage stopped in front of Cliff House, and Diane Page stepped down from it. She was ravishingly beautiful in a gown of softest cotton on which spring flowers ran riot; a wide bonnet with matching flowered ribbons sat on her golden curls. The lace edging of her sleeve fell back from one elegant white arm as she waved it languidly while issuing instructions to the driver about the two trunks strapped to the top of the carriage.

Miss Ettington, who had viewed this arrival from a parlor window, was standing at the door to greet her.

"My dear Mrs. Page, I did not expect you so soon."

Diane seemed to take this amiss. "Did you not get my letter?" she snapped.

"Two days ago . . . but you mentioned no date, and I thought . . ."

"I hope I am not inconveniencing you." Diane's haughty stare and satiric tone said that on the contrary, she didn't give a damn if she was.

"Oh, no . . . it was just the surprise. Vicky will be overwhelmed; she was so excited," the governess lied diplomatically. "And, of course, I haven't gotten in all the new supplies that we need, but I can just pop down to the village."

The driver dumped the trunks down in the hallway, bit down on the coin graciously handed him and went stomping out.

"I suppose," said Diane, barely waiting for his departure, "you mean you need more money.

That's always the first thing with you when I arrive."

As the mottled red of Miss Ettington's flush died away, she bit back her first hasty impulse to disclaim.

"Miss Vicky and I live in a very simple manner, Mrs. Page," she said with such false humility, she could hardly believe even so shallow and self-centered a woman as Diane would take her words at face value. "Naturally, *you* must have the best, and that costs more."

Diane, however, could accept any attitude or remark that seemed to elevate her. The lovely face softened; her luscious lips parted in a smile. She opened her purse and pressed several bills of generous amount into Miss Ettington's hands. "Get what you need," she urged, all benevolence. "I am in funds right now, even though . . ." A cloud settled over her face again.

I was right, thought Miss Ettington, *something is wrong*. She experienced that stab of fear again. She knew it wasn't wise, but she had to ask; she just had to.

"You haven't come for Miss Vicky, have you?" she blurted out, as tactlessly blunt as Vicky herself might have been.

"Come for Vicky," Diane repeated blankly.

Miss Ettington's hands tightened around the bills she was still holding, almost tearing them in two.

"To take her away to London."

"Good Lord, of course not!" Diane gasped, and Miss Ettington's breathing returned to normal. "As though I ever would. Especially," she finished bitterly, "after what just happened."

"What, dear Mrs. Page," asked Miss Ettington, prepared in her joy to be generous with words if nothing else, "was that?"

Diane seemed to consider for a moment, but the need to air her grievance outweighed all discretion. She flung herself into a chair, and the story poured out.

"I was visiting friends in Hampshire last week —the Portermans, you know, cousins of the duke of Tellfort. Sir Arthur Chillingsoworth was a guest there, too. You've heard of him, of course. His grandfather made a fortune in India, and his father actually increased it. Maria Porterman let me know at once that the man is looking about him for a wife. Well, one understands, of course. Naturally, he wants an heir for those estates, and though God knows I don't want— but he has simply *pots* of money, and I could see"—she preened herself like a peacock spreading its tail—"that the moment he set eyes on me, he was most *epris*. All through my visit he devoted himself to me; I was expecting a proposal any day."

She sat up, hands clasping and unclasping. "I couldn't understand what was holding him back until Maria gave me a hint. He thought that *I* might be a bit too long in the tooth to bear him a child. Can you believe it? The man's forty-five if he's a day, and I'm only twenty-n—" She looked at Miss Ettington, remembered the governess knew her true age, and admitted grudgingly, "So I'm thirty-one. As though that's too old to have a child!"

"So you came away?" Miss Ettington probed delicately.

"I should have. He might have relented and come after me." Her voice grew shrill and unlovely again. "Instead I told him the truth. I told him about Vicky."

"You did!" cried Miss Ettington with unflattering surprise, which fortunately passed Diane by.

"Well, I thought if he knew I had already had *one* child, he wouldn't worry so about my—my— and I did tell him that she lived apart from me and would continue to—but it had just the opposite effect I intended it to." A sullen frown creased the pretty face. "You never saw a man so frightened," she went on scornfully. "Even though I told him again and again about you and how absolutely *devoted* you are to Vicky, I could tell he was scared out of his wits that he might be called upon to maintain her . . . as though he couldn't afford to support a dozen stepdaughters without even noticing it. He made some excuse to the Portermans and was gone from the house the next day."

"If he was such a fainthearted man," said Miss Ettington, daring to place a comforting hand on her ex-pupil's shoulder, "then he just wasn't worthy of you, Mrs. Page."

Diane lifted her head, once more arrogant and assured. "Oh, I know that," she said with bravado. "Just the same, I'm not taking any chances in the future. I'll tie the next man up in a good safe matrimonial knot before ever he learns about Vicky."

Chapter Five

DIANE VICTORIA PAGE, ALL UNAWARE OF HER
mother's arrival at Cliff House, sat on the edge
of a dilapidated wooden pier, with one leg
crossed underneath her and the other raised up
to provide a prop for her sketching pad. Her
suntanned face was bent over the pad, the tip of
her tongue curled out between her lips, while
her skillful fingers flew across the page.

A shadow came over the book suddenly, blot-
ting out her light. She turned her head impatiently even as the boy behind her exclaimed,
"Oh, I say, that's very good for—"

His voice trailed away, the last tactless phrase
left unsaid. Obligingly, she said it for him.

"For a little girl?" she filled in.

He laughed ruefully. "I suppose everybody says that?"

"Yes, everybody does."

"I can see why you might mind. Actually, it's very good—for anyone."

He smiled at her so pleasantly, she couldn't help smiling back.

"Ack-shally," she said in almost comical despair, "it isn't good at all. I haven't got the—the—I don't know what it is, but something's missing."

He glanced down the beach toward a group of fishermen talking, arguing, gesticulating together. "It looks to me just like them." He gave this opinion cautiously, not wanting to offend her again.

"No, it doesn't. It's Mr. Llanwelly. He's different from every other one of them. He's the most special fisherman that ever was, and I can't get it so that it truly looks like him."

"You will one day. You need practice and perhaps a better drawing master than the one you have now."

She looked up into the sympathetic gray-green eyes and laughed merrily. "I don't have a drawing master *at all*."

"When you go to school, you will."

"Oh, I won't go to school. Aunt Etti can teach me everything I need to know. She used to be a governess."

The boy looked down at her, somewhat startled. He had a narrow, clever, plain but pleasant face, not too unlike her own, except that a life in the sun had darkened hers like a gypsy's and his was schoolroom-pale. He was by nature both intelligent and warmhearted, but thirteen years of privilege had left its inevitable mark. In his world no one announced relationship to a governess with quite such an air of pride.

"What's your name?" he asked.

"Vicky."

"For the queen?"

"I s'pose." She hunched an impatient shoulder at this oft-repeated question. "I was borned the day she got to be crowned."

"That makes you"—he paused a moment and used his fingers to help his calculations—"seven years and not quite two months old."

"My goodness. You figured that real fast." Her blue eyes blinked up at him admiringly. "How old are you?"

"Thirteen and a half—almost."

"Do you go to school?"

"Yes, Eton."

"You eat at school?" she asked, somewhat puzzled.

He stared at her, then his face broke out in a sudden bright smile. "No, Eton . . . E-T-O-N is the name of the school I go to."

"Do you like it?"

He took a cautious look around, then settled on the pier beside her, his arms around his knickered legs. "Not very much. You have to pretend

47

to like games or everyone thinks you're a swot. There's not enough good stuff to eat and far too much thrashing. I do have some jolly friends, though."

"It sounds like a horrid place." Vicky shuddered. "I can help myself to something in the kitchen whenever I'm hungry. And Aunt Etti doesn't believe in corp—corp—you know, hitting."

"I know," he grinned. "I wish I didn't." He added wistfully, "Oh, I can take a few licks. What I mind most is that they won't let me keep my bones there."

"Your *bones!*"

"The ones I've dug up from Grand Cavern; that's a huge cave on the northeast corner of my father's lands in Devonshire. It's the most amazingly splendid place. My father sent for a geologist—that means a man of science—to come from a society in London; and he said that our cave and lots of smaller ones around date from the Pleistocene period—that means hundreds of thousands or more years ago. And—oh, hell—oh Lord, I beg your pardon, Vicky for swearing and for boring you."

"I don't mind swearing. Mr. Llanwelly swears bee-yoo-tafully. And I don't understand lots of your words, but I'm not bored. I wish I did understand about Ples—Plus—"

"Pleistocene."

"What about the bones?"

"There are caves just full of them, layers and

layers, enough to fill a castle. Bones of the people who lived there long before we once thought the world began . . . bits of their tools and weapons and things from their households. . . ."

His pale face glowed with a passion Vicky could only vaguely comprehend until she realized, in a flash of intuition, that it was how she herself felt when one of her drawings came out just right.

She put her hand on his arm. Her voice was warm with sympathy. "It's mean that they won't let you have your bones at this Eton school, but if they've been buried in your cave so many years, then they'll still be waiting for you when you get out of school, won't they?" she asked practically.

He grinned. "You bet they will. And when I go up to Oxford—that's a higher school," he said before she could ask—"I'll study geology so I'll know what to do about them."

He hesitated a moment. "Look." He took a folded handkerchief from his knickers pocket and carefully unfolded it, holding out a small, slightly curved bone, knobby on one end. "This is the first fossil bone I ever found. Dr. Russell—the geologist—said it was probably a leg bone from a child." "Isn't it marvelous?" he asked, the radiance of knowledge so illuminating his gray-green eyes that Vicky found herself agreeing, in all honesty, "Oh, my, yes!"

He wrapped up the bone in his handkerchief

again, as gently as a mother covering her child, and restored it to his pocket.

"What I don't understand," Vicky pursued, frowning a little, "is why your family makes you go to that awful school. Don't they love you?"

He blushed beet red. "It's got nothing to do with love," he protested, unnerved by her unblinking stare. "My mother is dead, and my father," he quoted unconsciously, "wants me to be properly educated for my station in life."

"What's a station in life?" she inquired curiously.

He squirmed in embarrassment. "Well, I've got a brother, you see, but I'm—er—the older son."

"Being an older son is your station in life?"

"If your father is a lord, it is," he told her rather apologetically. "My father is the eighth Baron Vaile; I'll be the ninth."

"Your father is called a lord?"

"Yes, he's Lord Vaile."

"And you will be Lord Vaile, too, some day?"

He nodded, startled when she went off into peals of laughter. "You d-don't l-look at all like a l-lord," she chortled.

He stared across at her steadily. "Now we're quits," he said at last.

"Quits?"

"You didn't like it when I *almost* said you drew well for a little girl."

She bent her head over her pad once more, not drawing, just thinking. When she lifted her head, her face was overshadowed by the shame of his swift, subtle lesson in manners.

"I'm very *very* sorry," she said contritely. "Aunt Etti tells me all the time I should think before I speak. Are you angry with me?"

That sudden bright smile of his warmed her once again. "Not anymore, Vicky."

She smiled shyly back, offering the gift of her friendship as she did. "I like you, Lord Vaile," she told him.

"No, no," he explained quickly. "I'll only be Lord Vaile when my father dies, and I hope that's a long time away."

"Oh, my goodness, yes. What do I call you then?"

"I'm Rupert Vaile." He grinned again. "I was named after someone famous, too, Prince Rupert of Bavaria, who served Charles II during the Restoration. We're descended from him, sort of, only on the wrong side of—"

He broke off, recollecting all at once that, in spite of the wise young-monkey face and clear bright eyes, he was speaking to a seven-year-old.

"Wrong side of what?" she inquired perceptively.

He coughed as excuse to hide a reddened face behind one hand. "It doesn't matter," he muttered.

"That means it does matter, but you think I'm too young to know. Never mind," said Vicky serenely, "I'll ask Aunt Etti. She never says like other mothers"—her voice took on a mocking, mimicking tone—*"I'll explain when you're older."*

"Rupert. Ho, Rupert."

The shout came from the other end of the pier where a carriage now stood with a man standing in front of it, vigorously waving one arm.

"There's my father now. Come and meet him," Rupert urged.

Vicky got slowly to her feet, hugging the pad to her, but she hung back when Rupert took her arm.

"I better not," she said hesitantly.

"Oh, come on, I want to show him your pictures. He's an art collector, you know."

"He is!" At that, Vicky walked along quickly, though her shyness returned when they came close to Lord Vaile. Her memories of London were dim now, and she could not recollect ever having met such an elegant-looking man, even in the informality of his tweed trousers and a mustard frock coat, a gold watch chain stretched across his ample waist and a monocle seemingly screwed over the one eye bent so piercingly upon her.

"This is Vicky, father," Rupert introduced her. "Do look at her drawings."

"If I may," said Lord Vaile courteously enough but in such a penetrating voice, it made Vicky jump.

Mutely she held out her sketch pad, and he turned over the pages slowly and with genuine interest.

"Did you know you show great talent, my dear?" he asked her when he was done, and Rupert beamed with all the pride of a patron for his protégé.

"Yes, sir. I mean, yes, Lord Vaile," she corrected herself. "Aunt Etti has told me I do."

"You must get some training when you are older if you can," he pursued.

"Aunt Etti is trying to arrange it," she answered politely.

"Good. Come, Rupert." He turned toward his son. "Uncle Henry will be waiting dinner, and you know how cross that makes him." He turned back toward Vicky and lifted his hat. "Good-bye, little girl. Good luck to you."

Seeing her scowl, Rupert's shoulders lifted in mute apology for the "little girl."

"Tomorrow?" he mouthed as he moved off in his father's wake.

Vicky nodded vigorously.

As man and boy reached the end of the wharf and stepped toward the carriage, two women appeared along the road. They were a study in contrast, one of middle age with dulling hair and careworn face, wearing a drab gray gown relieved of its severity by only a small crocheted collar; the other a work of nature's art in rustling taffeta petticoats and sweeping skirts that were a riot of spring flowers, a becoming bonnet set on her golden curls and framing her willful but altogether lovely face.

Lord Vaile stopped instinctively with a connoisseur's appreciation of beauty, and in that second Diane's brilliant blue eyes met the more sober gray-green ones like his son's.

On her part, there was instant recognition.

"Why, Lord Vaile!" she trilled and stepped toward him, leaving Miss Ettington alone on the road. "Of all places to meet you. What a delightful surprise."

Her gloved hand stretched out; her eyes sparkled up at him.

He took the hand and bent to bring it to his lips. Wise in the ways of men, Diane knew he hadn't the foggiest notion who she was. Her full lips achieved an enchanting pout even as she retrieved her hand and held it against her deliberately heaving breast.

"Oh, you don't remember me, dear sir."

She sounded so young and sweet and flustered that Lord Vaile was moved to protest this obvious truth.

"My dear ma'am . . ."

"Diane Wellington-Ware," she prompted, peeping up at him. "We met—oh, my goodness, it must be ten years ago—at my coming-out party at my brother's house on Wimpole Street. Sir William Wellington-Ware, you know. I was *so* shy and frightened that night, and I have never forgotten how very kind and reassuring you were. . . ."

Lord Vaile now recollected the lady, if not the meeting, and in the face of her beaming good will was prepared to believe in his own long forgotten goodness.

"My dear Miss Wellington-Ware, of course—"

"Mrs. Page," she corrected gently. "I was married to Captain Harlan Page of Her Majesty's army, who gave his life for his country in India more than seven years past."

"My dear ma'am." Once again he took her gloved hand, this time to press it comfortingly. "What you must have endured . . . I, too, lost my wife some years since."

Diane, who knew of his loss quite well and also that he had not yet remarried, uttered aloud cries of sorrow for him even as she concealed her inward delight.

They were alone now, for Miss Ettington, knowing her presence was not only superfluous but unwanted, had gone past them to step up on the pier and walk to the end of the dock where Vicky sat, drawing once again.

Bored, unnoticed, Rupert promptly followed her.

"Do you have property here in Cornwall, Lord Vaile?" Diane was inquiring prettily of the father as the son departed.

"No, but my Uncle Henry lives near here, a dear old man but inclined to exaggerate his illnesses. For the past decade, at least two or three times a year, when he grows lonely, I receive a summons to his deathbed. By the second day of the visit, he is sitting up in bed demanding cigars and port; by the third, he is at the dinner table, eating so prodigiously as to bring on a genuine bilious attack."

"How kind of you to be so understanding." Diane's laughter was warm with approval; it was also—as she had countless times been told—a merry, musical sound.

Lord Vaile smiled in appreciation. "And you, Mrs. Page? Is this where you reside now?"

"Oh, no. Like you"—her appealing blue eyes lifted up to his for a moment, then were modestly cast down—"I, too, am here on a mission of mercy. Once or twice a year I visit my old governess, Miss Ettington. I gave her Cliff House on the Ramston Road for her retirement after she was pensioned off."

Diane waved her hand toward the end of the wharf where, for the first time, he observed that the little girl who sketched so well, the drab-looking female in gray and his heir were all grouped together.

"Oh, your Miss Ettington must be the Aunt Etti that raggedy little girl spoke of."

"Er—yes—she is." Diane felt her way cautiously, concealing her fright.

"I spoke to the child for a few moments and looked at her drawings. She has amazing talent for one of her background. She should have instruction."

"So Miss Ettington has told me," said Diane, her lips now drooping pathetically. "But to house and feed and clothe them both . . . and my resources are so slim. I try to contrive, but"—she looked up at him sadly—"I was not left well off, you know, and my brother and I were estranged over my marriage. He wanted me to accept Lord Fortescue's proposal at the time I became betrothed to my husband."

"Lord Fortescue! That revolting rakish leftover from the Regency! I am surprised at Sir William."

"William was ambitious for me," sighed Diane. "I tried not to blame him, but mine was a marriage of affection."

"More honor to you, dear lady," declared Lord Vaile staunchly as he looked toward the wharf again. "And you support them both," he marveled, "at no small sacrifice to yourself, I am sure."

"I had to give up my house," Diane admitted, "but I do not repine. I have a charming set of rooms, and what need have I for more, just me and my faithful old maid?"

Lord Vaile possessed himself of both her hands and once more pressed them comfortingly. "How sad that you never had children," he pursued. "My boys are my greatest comfort, especially my heir . . ." He indicated the knickered boy at the end of the wharf.

Rupert now sat with his legs dangling over the dock, contentedly watching over the girl beside him, busy with her sketching.

The deep sigh Diane fetched up from her diaphragm swelled her breast halfway out of her bodice. Lord Vaile, having admired the effect, tore his eyes away to ask abruptly, "Miss Ettington is the child's aunt?"

"So she says, and I accept it."

"You mean—?"

"Who am I to judge?" queried Diane softly. "She is called her aunt and treats her dearly as any daughter." She moistened her lips and took the final step along the road to concealment. "Dear Etti's Vicky has been like my own child to me."

As moved as he was intrigued, Lord Vaile once again took hold of both her hands. "My dear Mrs. Page," he told her with pompous sincerity, "the beauty of your face is exceeded only by the nobility of your character."

"Oh, Lord Vaile!" Diane allowed him to see the blushes suffusing her pink cheeks before she turned away her head in modest confusion.

I've got him, she exulted inwardly. *Praise God, I've got him!*

Chapter Six

DIANE CAME DOWN THE STAIRS OF CLIFF HOUSE as her daughter skipped toward the front door.

"Where are you going, Vicky?"

"To the wharf."

"To meet Rupert Vaile, I suppose?" Diane said in quick alarm.

A sullen mask descended over Vicky's face. "Yes," she said. Her replies to her mother this past week had all been equally short, sharp and defiant.

Diane nibbled her lips in worry. "I really wish you wouldn't," she declared fretfully.

Vicky shrugged, then said slyly, "He might come here if I didn't. He knows where I live."

"Oh, very well." Diane shrugged her annoyance. "Why he bothers with a child like you . . . but I suppose he has nothing else to do in this deadly place." She added placatingly, "Vicky dear, *do* remember what I told you," and placed a light hand on her daughter's shoulder. Vicky bore the weight of it in Spartan silence for a few seconds, then moved out from under the delicate fingertips.

"I shan't forget," she returned stolidly. "Aunt Etti is *really* my aunt, and *you* visit us because she was your governess. I am not to call you mother in front of anyone."

Having finished this recital, Diane Victoria Page, aged seven, walked to the door and opened it wide, then turned back to look at Diane Wellington-Ware Page, thirty-one.

"You need not worry," the younger Diane said with awful, unnatural dignity. "I shall make sure never to call you mother again."

Two days later an elaborate crested carriage stopped on the narrow pebbled path outside Cliff House.

While his father sat in dignity within and a footman advanced up the path, as directed, to bring down Mrs. Page's trunks, Rupert, having exchanged a few brief words with Miss Ettington, tore around to the garden in the back. Vicky knelt there, bending over a rosebush.

"Weren't you going to come and say good-bye to me, Vicky? That's mighty rude of you when you knew I was here!" he told her indignantly.

"I gave Aunt Etti a present for you," came a muffled voice.

"I know. She gave it to me. Are you crying?"

"Of course not. Do you like it?"

"I haven't looked at it yet." He tugged at the knotted ribbons on the rolled-up scroll that had been handed him. "I can't seem to get these loose. Oh, there—by George . . . I *say*, Vicky, this is—this is—it's really *me!*"

"Stupid, of course it's you."

"I don't know how to thank you, Vicky, for such an extra-special gift." He addressed the back of her neck. "It would be easier if you looked at me when I did."

Vicky stood up and turned around. Her face was dirt-streaked and tearstained; her eyes were red and puffy from crying.

"Vicky, what's the matter?" he asked in innocent concern.

She shot him a furious look for not knowing.

"You're going away, and I'll prob-ally never see you again."

"I'll visit Uncle Henry again with my dad, I'm sure I will," he said uncomfortably, then added on sudden inspiration, "And I tell you what, I'll get this picture of me framed, so I can hang it in my room at home. That way I'll be able to think of you whenever I look at it," he promised.

She gave such a woeful sniff, it smote his kind heart.

"I have a present for you, too, Vicky," he said, and before he could regret the generous impulse, he put his hand in his breeches pocket and drew out the bundled handkerchief. Under her wondering eyes, he unfolded it again, displaying the small curved bone with its one knobby end.

He pressed the bone, still swaddled in his handkerchief with the monogrammed RV in one corner, into her hands. "I want you to have it," he said. "Now you'll have something that will make *you* remember *me*."

Her blue eyes were alive and dancing; her dark gypsy face shone with delight. "But it's your most preciousest possession!"

"I want you to have it."

"Mr. Rupert." They had not heard the footman approach or open the garden gate. "Your father says it is time to leave."

Rupert closed her fingers over the fossil. "Good-bye, Vicky," he said. "Take care of it for me."

She had resolved to stay in the garden till the sound of the carriage wheels died away, but at the last moment her strength of will gave way. She came tearing toward the road as the coachman raised his whip and Rupert leaned out his head to shout, "Good-bye, Vicky. Thanks for my picture."

She called back her own good-byes, dancing up and down so excitedly that Miss Ettington took her by the hand to make sure she did not tumble into the path of the carriage.

Lord Vaile just barely raised his hat and Diane inclined her head, every inch the lady of the manor.

She really is anticipating, Miss Ettington thought wryly, even as she lightly pinched Vicky's elbow so the child would join her in a slight curtsey as the carriage bowled by.

Still, Miss Ettington knew of old that what Miss Diane wanted, Miss Diane usually got, so the letter from Derbyshire only three months later came as no great surprise to her.

It was written in a sprawling, scrawling hand that would have disgraced a ten-year-old and signed with a grand flourish, *Lady Vaile.* Diane wrote sentimentally of the quick and quiet wedding that had taken place within four weeks after her departure from Cornwall.

"My dear Thomas was in such a hurry to claim me and carry me into Derbyshire, I had not the heart to refuse him," she boasted, and Miss Ettington smiled ironically, knowing who had been in the greater hurry. "Such jewels and clothes as he has heaped on me, as well as a new carriage of my own because I have so many calls to make and return. Needless to say, as the wife of the most important landowner hereabouts, I have been accorded all the courtesy and homage that is my due."

"You need not worry about your own future either," Diane continued loftily. "Mr. Saxon will send your allowance, as he has always done, but since my husband knows nothing of this—*nor must he know*—you will also receive a quarterly sum from Lord Vaile. He has most generously decided that, as my old governess, you should receive a pension."

Ah, she must have told him she had been paying me one, Miss Ettington decided, grateful but cynical.

After rejoicing at some length that her husband not only outranked her brother, the baronet, but was by far the richer man, Diane wound up her letter on an anxious note.

"If you ever need to contact me, you must do so under cover to Mr. Saxon, never direct to my home here in Derbyshire or to our London house. My husband is rather old-fashioned in some respects. The daily mail comes first to him, and he reads it all before it is handed out. I cannot count on privacy, so if you write to me here, you must never say anything out-of-the-way. Of course, I have every intention of telling him about Vicky one day, but I will have to delay till the time is right. So please give my darling child my fondest love and tell her that I have sent her an exquisite French doll and some lovely dresses as well as a box full of drawing materials from London. You will know how to make her understand that now that I am Lady Vaile, I will not be able to visit her so often as before."

"So often as before," jeered Miss Ettington under her breath, then aloud, "That bitch."

But even as she spoke, her heart rejoiced. Their life at Cliff House was safe; she was secure with Vicky. She knew her Diane. Oh, how she knew her. The visits would be few and far between and finally fade away to nothing. The communications would dwindle down to the quarterly checks from Mr. Saxon as well as the new husband.

"Vicky," she said that evening as they sat over their simple supper of vegetable soup, bread and cheese, with some apple tarts she had baked for dessert, "I have some news for you."

Vicky looked up expectantly.

"Your mother has married Lord Vaile."

"I thought she was being extra sugary-sweet to him," said Vicky without any change of expression. "I s'pose that's the way to behave when you want to marry someone."

"I sup-pose," Miss Ettington faltered, greatly taken aback.

A slight frown creased Vicky's forehead. "Will it make any difference to us, Aunt Etti?" she asked.

"How do you mean, Vicky?"

"Ohh, visits . . . and money."

"There'll be plenty of money," Miss Ettington assured her swiftly, "more than we've ever had before. And your mother is sending you some splendid presents from London, dresses and a French doll"—Vicky snorted—

"and"—she paused impressively—"some drawing materials."

Vicky brightened. "Then I'm glad she married him," she observed matter-of-factly.

"But since Mrs. Page is a married lady and must stay with her husband"—Miss Ettington hunted desperately in her mind for an unhurting way to phrase this—"she may not be able to visit as often as she used to."

Vicky bit down on the flaky crust of her tart. "That's good," she commented calmly, with her mouth full. "We'll be much happier without her, and now you can be my real mother."

Miss Ettington stared at the child, mouth agape, sudden rare tears standing in her eyes.

Vicky hastily swallowed a mouthful of apple and came running around the table.

"I thought you wanted to be," she soothed the governess. "Please don't cry, Aunt Etti."

"I want it m-more than anything," Miss Ettington stammered childishly, "but your m-mother—"

"You heard her yourself telling me not to call her mother anymore. She told me over and over." The child's face hardened. "And I never will," she vowed.

Miss Ettington stilled the voice of conscience. What loyalty did she owe Diane? What loyalty did either of them owe her?

"I would like to be your mother, Vicky." Even as she said the wonderful words, she gave a brisk nod of her head to make it seem a casual decision.

Vicky frisked joyfully around the table, then sat down again. Her gurgle of laughter—had she but known it—sounded much like Diane, Lady Vaile's musical trill. "I shall call you mama," she said decidedly.

"Then your first duty as my daughter," Miss Ettington told her, very solemn, "is to start taking unpleasant orders."

Vicky stared across at her anxiously.

"No more apple tarts till you have finished your soup."

"Yes, mama." Vicky grinned engagingly and lifted her soup spoon. They were both silent until she had drained the last drop from her bowl and reached for a second tart.

"You know, mama," she said very thoughtfully, again with her mouth full. "Maybe you should try being sugary-sweet with Mr. Llanwelly."

"Vicky!"

"Well, I'd rather have him for my da than Lord Vaile, and just think, if you married up with him, I would get three brothers."

Miss Ettington, very red of face, murmured that she was not thinking of marrying anyone.

"No?" said Vicky, her eyes innocently wide and her mouth pursed up, angelically sweet.

"No!" said Miss Ettington rather too forcefully.

"Then you needn't," Vicky conceded generously. "Can I have another tart, mama?"

"Yes, dear," said Miss Ettington absently, her mind far away.

Before her "mother" could realize that this was tart number three, Vicky helped herself quickly to the last one on the plate.

Chapter Seven

ON DIANE VICTORIA PAGE'S EIGHTH BIRTHDAY, she was excused from lessons and Miss Ettington packed a huge picnic basket for her to take down to the village school so she could share her birthday lunch with her best friends and would-be brothers, Peter, Powys and Patric Llanwelly.

What Miss Ettington did not know was that the Llanwelly boys were meeting Vicky, not in the schoolyard but on the rocks a safe half-mile from Cliff House. They would all walk together the rest of the way to their favorite isolated cove along the shore, a truancy that had been planned a full two weeks before.

The village school would be closing for the summer in only a few days, so what, they had all agreed, did this one afternoon matter? Prudently, however, they refrained from mentioning their plans to Vicky's mother, the boys' father and especially not to the schoolmaster, Mr. Nealey, whose level of tolerance was low. He was prone to use his birch and ask questions afterward.

"Even da might not be best pleased," admitted Peter, the oldest of the four, as they lay stretched out on the sand, pleasantly tired from a game of tag among the rocks, happily replete from lunch. The overhang of a huge boulder protected them from the direct rays of the sun, but it was hot . . . and she was stretched out so comfortably. . . . With the murmur of the boys' voices in her ears, Vicky fell asleep.

She was roused by a loud shout from the shore and sat up, rubbing her eyes. The boys, all of them, in clinging wet underdrawers, were at the far end of the shore.

"Pigs!" she yelled. They had gone for their first swim without her!

Having kicked off her shoes and stockings before lunch, she had only to strip herself of her dimity dress, cotton petticoat and skimpy chemise, leaving on just her pink cotton drawers.

"Pigs!" she shouted again, racing along the beach to the Llanwelly boys. "Why didn't you wake me up before you went swimming?" she reproached them.

"Never mind that. You'll never guess what we found," said Powys impressively. He was the nearest of the boys in age to her but always made a big thing of being three months older.

"I don't want to guess. Tell me."

"No, guess, guess," piped up six-year-old Patric.

"Oh, crikey!" burst out Peter. "Get on with it, do!" He then proceeded to tell her himself. "We were swimming a bit farther outside the cove, and we found an old smugglers' cave."

"A smugglers' cave!" Vicky breathed in awe. "How do you know?"

"There was a sunken boat there and whiskey bottles lying all around, most of them broken, but look at this one." He pointed to the bottle lying in the sand, and Vicky dropped down to her knees, sniffing at it.

"I just smell the sea," she said disappointedly.

"It's brandy. I'm sure of it."

Vicky jumped up. "Oh, show me the cave. Maybe there's other things there; maybe there's real treasure."

She raced toward the water, the three boys pelting after her.

"I don't know." Peter put his hand on her shoulder, feeling the sudden responsibility of his eleven years. "Maybe we shouldn't till we speak to da. It's a tricky swim."

"Oh, don't be silly, Peter. I swim as good as any of you . . . oh, well," she conceded, "at least as good as Powys and Patric. *You* taught me, didn't you? And how can we tell your father without him finding out"—she flung her arms wide in a gesture that encompassed the sun, the sand, the water and the picnic basket—"about this?"

"All right. But keep close to me, and do whatever I say." She nodded happily. "And you two," he admonished his brothers, "stay right here and wait for us. Understand?" They nodded solemnly.

Peter and Vicky swam in the surf, bobbing about like porpoises till he stopped her with a gesture and pointed down. "It's right below here. Take a deep breath and stay right next to me."

They both gulped in huge amounts of air before diving beneath the water, Vicky making sure to keep in touching distance of Peter.

The smugglers' cave was shallow and easy to find. She kicked around over the sunken boat, poking about but finding no buried treasure. Something shiny seemed to be sticking out of the rocks that formed the rounded back of the cave. She reached out as Peter indicated it was time for them to leave.

There was a rumbling sound, dirt and gravel and spray filled up her eyes and nose, strangling her; her lungs were bursting. She felt Peter reaching for her and, in her panic, tried frantically to get her arms around him.

She never saw his fist lash out; there was a second of sharp pain, then nothing. When her eyes cleared, and her head, and she became aware of the world around her once more, they were almost to the beach again. Peter had her by her hair, wrapped around his hand, and Powys and Patric had swum out to help him.

They all lay exhausted at the shore. Only when Powys said, "We'll get too burned by the sun," did they return to the shade of the over-hanging boulder.

There was some lemonade left in the picnic basket. It was warm, but they shared it thankfully.

"What happened?" Vicky asked after a while.

"The cave wall collapsed. I guess we disturbed it too much. The whole thing just about came down on us."

"Did I get hit by a rock?" Gingerly she caressed her jaw.

"No, I punched you. I had to, Vicky, you were strangling me. I had to get us both out of there."

"You saved us both then," she told him solemnly. "Thank you, Peter. Don't worry about the punch."

"I'm the oldest. I shouldn't have let you be there in the first place. That's what da will say."

"We don't have to tell him!" Vicky cried, aghast. "Let it be our secret. All of our secret."

Peter shook his head. "No," he repeated stubbornly. "I'm the oldest. We have to tell him."

So, some two hours later, they stood in front of Mr. Llanwelly, the four of them, stumbling and stammering over their confession.

The fisherman's face seemed to be carved out of granite during the whole of their halting recital.

When he spoke, it was in his usual slow, calm way. "On a fine hot June day, I can understand your wanting to play truant, though it's supperless you'll go to bed for it all the same."

The boys exchanged quick glances of relief. After their generous picnic lunch, supperless to bed was not too bad a fate.

Then Mr. Llanwelly spoke in a voice that made them all jump.

"What I find hard to forgive," he rapped out, "is your forgetting every lesson of the sea I ever taught you. Respect it, fear it, make friends with it, but never ever forget there's danger waiting in it always, if you grow careless or forgetful. You risked your lives, the four of you, like foolish city folk who never came near or nigh the ocean. I'm not only angry, I'm ashamed of you. So here's a lesson to remind you."

Starting with his youngest, Patric, Mr. Llanwelly upended each boy and walloped away at his backside with a hard calloused palm, increasing the strength of his blows when he came to eight-year-old Powys and preserving his best efforts for his oldest son.

Vicky stood there, helpless and shocked, with her hands half-covering her face so as not to shame them, while the boys remained stoically silent throughout, glad to have it so soon over. Da had reason on his side, they acknowledged, and any other father around would have most probably used his thick leather belt. Vicky, unaware of these niceties of calculation, wept profusely throughout their ordeal and was totally unprepared for her own.

"It's time you had a lesson, too, young lady. It's spoiled you are, and feckless, and happen if your ma won't do something about it, then someone must."

Before she could cry out or protest, a heavy hand clamped onto her shoulder and Vicky found herself turned swiftly about. Three hard stinging smacks were delivered to her bottom with a speed that made her head spin round.

"You three off home to bed," Mr. Llanwelly directed his sons. "You, miss, follow me." And he set off at a brisk pace down the road with Vicky, lugging the picnic basket, lagging behind him.

Halfway to Cliff House, Mr. Llanwelly turned his head. Silent tears streaked down Vicky's face as she staggered wearily along, stumbling over her own feet, the basket almost dragging on the ground.

She stared back at him defiantly. They both knew only her stubborn pride kept her upright.

Without a word he swooped down on her and scooped her, basket and all, up into his arms. She curled thankfully against him, her head on his shoulder.

"Lassie, lassie," he said against her hair, "you might ha' drowned! Could I have ever faced

Miss Ettington again if aught happened to you in the charge of my own sons?"

Vicky didn't answer. He thought she had fallen asleep, but presently she lifted her head so she could peer into his face.

"You like my mama, don't you?"

"Aye." His cheeks reddened.

"She likes you, too." Vicky shook her head. "I don't understand."

"What don't you understand, lass?"

"If you like each other, why do neither of you act sugary-sweet, the way Diane did with Lord Vaile? Then you could get married."

"Lord Vaile is a gentleman and your mother a lady. It's different with gentlefolk. They belong together. Like marries like."

"I still don't understand."

"Miss Ettington and you—you're gentlefolk, too—educated, nice-talking. I'm naught but a common fisherman. I can read and write and cipher a bit, but I wouldn't know how to behave outside this village. Caroline—Miss Ettington— she comes from a world I've never even seen, let alone could understand."

"That's silly," said Vicky. "Mama never wants to leave this village, she told me so. Nor do I. You should ask *her* how she feels."

With a tired sigh, she put her head back on his shoulder and fell asleep, not waking till she was tucked up in her own bed in a clean flowered nightgown, with Miss Ettington gently washing her dirt-streaked face with a warm soapy cloth.

"Did Mr. Llanwelly go home?" she asked sleepily.

"Yes. Oh, Vicky." She burst into tears. "You could have died!"

"Ouch! You got soap in my eyes."

"Good. You deserve it. You deserve worse. I wish Mr. Llanwelly had spanked you harder."

"It wasn't hard at all, not like the boys." Vicky giggled. "And he was *so* sorry, I could tell. Mama, he says he's too common for you. Why don't you tell him he isn't?"

"Because it's not a woman's place to tell a man. He's supposed to ask her."

"I think you're both silly," said Vicky.

"Vicky, don't be impertinent!"

"I'm not. You *always* tell me it's silly not to try to explain feelings to people. And this is feelings, isn't it?"

Miss Ettington stared down at the small determined face against the pillows. "Out of the mouth of babes and sucklings," she said slowly, which to Vicky made no sense at all.

She fell asleep still trying to figure out why mama had suddenly looked so pleased.

Chapter Eight

HE CAME, AS ALWAYS, WHEN SHE SENT FOR HIM, and they stood in her garden together.

"How old are you, Mr. Llanwelly?" she began the conversation.

"Thirty-nine, Miss Ettington, come Michaelmas Eve."

"I'm forty-two, and I've never been married."

"So I understand, ma'am. How—"

"But I've been with men. . . . Do you understand what I'm telling you?"

"Aye, I do, but—"

"Not just one man, men."

He said quietly, "Happen before my Annie, I tumbled a few wenches in my time, and I've not been quite a monk all the long years since she died."

"Did you do it for money?"

"For money?" he repeated slowly.

"I lay with men for their money."

"Why would you do that?"

She gave a short, angry laugh. "Why else but that I needed to? I was hungry and out of work. I had sold or pawned everything I owned except the clothes on my back. I decided I would rather be with a man, any man, than starve to death. So I did it. Every night for weeks—until I found —more acceptable work."

"Why are you telling me this, Caroline Ettington?"

"Because I'm tired of hearing from you about my gentility . . . and you the common fisherman. Do you still think I'm gentlefolk, Egan Llanwelly? I'm older than you and considerably soiled. Am *I* perhaps now too common for the likes of you?"

He took her by the shoulders and shook her, swearing as he did some fine rolling fishermens' oaths.

"Never say that again. You're a lady. Nothing in your past could make you less a lady."

"Ah, Egan," she said breathlessly when he was done with shaking her, "but am I *your* lady?"

He stepped toward her again. This time the hands that clasped her shoulders were loving and gentle.

"It seems that you have got to be because it's entirely worn out I am, trying to resist having you for my own."

"It—it doesn't have to be marriage," she said on a whisper and then stepped backward at the dark look he turned on her.

"Never say that again," he warned. "Now come here, woman."

His hand under her chin tipped up her face. Smiling, he bent his lips to hers.

After a while he lifted his head and looked at her a bit questioningly.

"I'm sorry," she said, color high. "I know it's a strange admission after what I just told you, but I haven't been kissed since I was a girl of twenty. The men who buy a woman's body for a quick coupling are not much interested in kisses."

With one rough hand he smoothed her gray-streaked hair, sending shivers of delight down her back. "I'll teach you," he said in his slow, quiet way. "It will be my pleasure. I'll make you forget the bad times. It *was* bad, wasn't it, lass?"

"Well," she said carefully, "no matter what the moralists say, it wasn't a fate worse than death. If it were, then obviously, I would have chosen to die. But, yes, you might say it was bad."

He kissed her wrists and the palms of her hands, then turned her hands over and let his lips drift along her knuckles, down to her very fingertips.

"I'll show you how good it can be, love," he promised gently. "We'll post the banns on Sunday."

Three weeks later they were married in the village church. The day before the ceremony Mr. Llanwelly hired a farm cart to move all of his and his sons' scant possessions from their fishing shack up to Cliff House.

The attic the boys would now share was bigger than their whole house had been, finer than any room they had ever seen. They tiptoed, awed, through the small dining parlor. Imagine, a separate room just to eat in. A kitchen with a big stone fireplace. And a parlor with the new gas lamps.

Only Vicky rebelled, going off into a tantrum when she discovered that she was expected to stay in the large best room with the big fourposter, while Mr. Llanwelly shared her mama's smaller room with its more modest bed.

"You said we were going to be a family, a real family! You lied to me!" she stormed, dashing for the door.

Egan Llanwelly caught hold of her as she tried to get through, and held her, struggling and kicking, till she exhausted herself.

When she had subsided in a sobbing heap, he demanded softly but sternly, "Now Vicky love, tell me what this is all about."

"You said we were going to be a family, but it's all pretend, like it always is," she said in a tight strained voice. "If we were really a family, then you would have the big room . . . the mother and father *always* do. Diane always took it when she came visiting. We're not really a family, are we? It's pretend, like"—she looked at the new Mrs. Llanwelly—"like I pretend you're my mama?"

"Oh Vicky, of course—"

"The girl's in the reet of it," Mr. Llanwelly interrupted firmly. "Happen, I should have thought of it myself. Of course, the mother and father should have the best room. It's not proper at all a little snip of a girl should have all this space to herself while her parents are so crowded."

He smiled to himself as he said it, for the smaller bedroom was bigger than any one he had ever seen, but with his quick sensitivity, he knew this had to be made right for Vicky, child of privilege, who in many ways had been less fortunate than his own boys.

"Bustle about, lass," he told his new wife with a twinkle in his eye. "Let's change over."

Bewildered, but happy, she started emptying out drawers.

Vicky came close to Mr. Llanwelly. "There's another thing," she confided, still tearful. "The boys are going to call mama Aunt Etti. Can I call you Uncle Egan?"

"If you want," he smiled. "Though, happen, da would be even better if you're going to take me for your father."

Vicky swallowed hard. "I would like that," she

said carefully. "But then—then—can't my name be Llanwelly, too, same as everyone else's in the house?"

"Surely it can," he agreed heartily.

When Vicky ran out at once, screeching for Peter, Powys and Patric, to tell them this grand piece of news, Egan said to his wife with passion, as though she had argued against him, "Where's the harm of it? Who's to know? Her father's dead. Her mother could not care less. By the time she's old enough to realize that it isn't lawful, she can do as she damn pleases."

"You're a good man, Egan Llanwelly," Caroline said softly as they each carried a pile of clothing into their new bedroom.

He smiled down into his wife's shining face. "I hope," he told her, his eyes merry and teasing, "you can still say the same in the morning after a night in this fine big bed our daughter gave us."

Caroline hid her blushes behind another pile of clothes.

"Are you shy with me, lass?"

"L-like a virgin," she mumbled.

"If you've never been with a man you cared for . . . ." He stopped to look at her questioningly, and she shook her head in vigorous denial . . . "then you *are* a virgin. Don't worry, Caroline love. Come the night, all will be well with us."

His hands caressed one of the bedposts; he looked wistfully out of the window at the blazing sun. "Caroline love," he repeated longingly, and she moved hastily toward the door, shaking her head.

"No, Egan, we daren't. The children would be sure to come back just at—just when—"

"In the very middle, you're reet. It's a way, you'll discover, that children have. But it's going to be a long, long day, love."

"For me, too, *love*," she mimicked fondly just as Vicky came clattering back up the stairs.

"Mama! Da!" she shrieked joyously. "I've got a *whole* new name. The boys and I decided. I'm not Diane Victoria Page anymore. I'm Page Caroline Llanwelly!" she announced triumphantly.

As they stared at her, dumbfounded, she hopped up and down in her excitement. "Do you understand how it works?" she demanded of them. "Page is for my first father, and that gives me a *P* name like my brothers. Peter, Powys, Patric and Page," she recited rapidly. "Doesn't it sound splendorful? And, of course, Caroline's for you, mama," she explained kindly, "and Llanwelly for my new father. You'll remember not to call me Vicky any more, won't you? I never did like being named for that fat lady queen. You won't forget my name is Page now?"

"Of course, Vicky," said Caroline, rather shaken.

"Thank you, mama."

Egan smothered a smile at this mutual lapse of memory. "We'll try to remember, Page," he told her gravely.

"Thank you, da. Is it all right," she asked importantly, "if my brothers and me take some pie and fruit and go down to the shore for a while? No smugglers' cave, I promise. We'll be careful."

"Take whatever you want," Egan told her fervently, moving toward the bed. "Stay as long as you want."

"What your dad means," said Caroline, bright red and slightly incoherent, "is you can stay as late as you want till it's supper time."

"Aye," agreed Egan, poker-faced, as he patted a pillow. "That was what I meant."

Chapter Nine

The London Times: Born, October 10, 1846, at their London residence, a daughter, Elizabeth Anne, to Lord and Lady Vaile of Landsdowne Hall, Derbyshire. By his first lady (who died 1842) Lord Vaile, who is eighth baron in the direct line, has two sons, Rupert and Marcus. Lady Vaile is the daughter of the late Sir Reginald Wellington-Ware.

The London Times: Born November 17, 1848, at Landsdowne Hall, Derbyshire, a second daughter, Emily Jane, to Diane (nee Wellington-Ware) Vaile, wife of Oliver, the eighth Baron Vaile.

AN UNFORGOTTEN LOVE

Eton
May 19, 1849

Dear Vicky,

My father broke his journey home to spend a day here with my brother Marcus and me on his way back from our Uncle Henry's funeral in Cornwall. He explained to me about having stopped by one afternoon before he left St. Ives to call on your aunt—Miss Ettington, wasn't that her name?—which he thought would please my stepmother, who appears to be devoted to her.

Imagine my surprise and pleasure when Father mentioned that he had gotten to see you as well and that you had asked that he bring me another picture.

I am delighted with the new drawing, Vicky. That old fossil bone of mine really comes alive in it. And the folds of the handkerchief... even to my tiny initials in the corner. To think of your having kept both just as I gave them to you all those years ago. Nearly four, isn't it?

I showed your drawing to one of the masters here, and he said that it is more than good, it shows an extraordinary if untutored talent. Do you understand what that means? That, though without formal training, you already show rare ability!

I am touched both by the present of the

drawing and your kindness in remembering me and sending me one on a subject so close to my heart. I shall keep it always just as I do your sketch of me, which hangs in my bedroom at Landsdowne Hall.

Now that Uncle Henry is gone, it is unlikely we will be coming into Cornwall again, but I hope that nonetheless I will meet you again one day. Or, at the very least, come across one of your paintings hanging in a gallery. Then I will be able to say to whatever companion I am with, I knew that artist when she was a barefoot girl sketching on a pier.

My very best wishes to you, always,

Rupert Vaile

Landsdowne Hall
Derbyshire
June 14, 1850

Dear Miss Ettington,

I ordered the set of paints, the sketching pads and the wooden easel to be sent from London in time for Vicky's birthday. Also three of the books you suggested. Why on earth does she want the one on fossils? Just like my stepson Rupert always occupied with his mouldy old bones. Morbid, I call it. I do hope you aren't encouraging her to turn into a bluestocking. Nothing repels men more!

AN UNFORGOTTEN LOVE

I know I said I would visit this summer for her birthday, but it really is just as impossible now as the two summers when I was enceinte. Oliver—Lord Vaile, that is—always insists on our going to Derbyshire in late spring and never leaving it before mid-autumn.

He thinks it healthier for all the children, his sons who come during the school holidays and our daughters as well. He has this obsession about the fresh country air. Indeed, some of his notions are hopelessly old-fashioned. I have a wonderful nanny and a perfectly competent nursery maid, but he insists (aided and abetted, I make no doubt, by his relic of a mother, old Lady Vaile, who lives at the Dower House) that a woman should be in constant supervision of her own nursery.

Since Uncle Henry died last year, there is really not much in the way of excuse I can give for taking the long journey to Cornwall. Oliver has a strong sense of what is due old family retainers and would understand my wanting to visit my former governess but not to the neglect of my own family. Family, according to him, is the very cornerstone of the empire. Too, too excessive at times.

If you explain to Vicky, I am sure she will understand what has kept me away all this time. And, of course, if it weren't for my marriage, she wouldn't have all those luxuries I send her . . . the lovely clothes, all the books and drawing materials, the hampers of fine foods from Fortnum's, the gold bracelet last Christmas.

I am sure I can rely on you to know exactly how to tell her.

*Yours very truly,
Diane, Lady Vaile*

*Law Offices
Saxon, Carruthers, & Wheale
London
November 13, 1851*

Miss Caroline Ettington
Cliff House on the Ramston Road
St. Ives, Cornwall

My dear Madam,

I must apologize for the long delay in replying to your letter. I refer to yours of October first, addressed to my uncle, Barnaby Saxon, who I regret to inform you died four weeks ago of a heart ailment he had suffered under for some six years.

As soon as the unexpected press of business permitted, I gave due diligence to a study of the Page file, which now comes into my hands as a trustee in conjunction with the bank.

There appears to be nothing unreasonable about your request for a small increase in the quarterly stipend for the upkeep of Cliff House. There has been none at all, I noted, since you and young Miss Diane took occupation about eight years ago, which means that you have lived most frugally during that entire period.

The spirit of the law must be considered as well as the letter, and I am sure that such an increase would have the approbation of the late Commander Page. He would wish his granddaughter to live at Cliff House, which is to be hers hereafter, with every reasonable comfort that his legacy allows. It is my opinion that any rational need of hers should be granted so long as the body of the principal is not attached, which is far from being the case. Instead, every year, a sum from the interest has been added to it.

Lady Vaile was notified immediately of my uncle's passing and has requested that we continue, as before, to act as go-between in all affairs concerning her daughter.

In the event of any emergency, you may telegraph. All future inquiries or instructions may come to me.

With all respect, madam—and my uncle several times spoke of his vast respect for you—I am yours to command at any time.

Yours very truly,
George Leonard Wheale, Solicitor

AN UNFORGOTTEN LOVE

Cliff House
St. Ives, Cornwall
May 4, 1852

Dear Mr. Wheale,

By the happiest chance, I have lately learned that Jean Pierre Charmont, a modern French painter, not much known in England but greatly renowned in his own land, Normandy, is sojourning in St. Ives—not the village but the town—for the next two to three months.

It was too great an opportunity to miss. Unknown to her, I took a portfolio of Miss Page's paintings to him in hopes that he would be willing to instruct her. I daresay Lady Vaile may never have mentioned that her daughter has outstanding talent as an artist.

Mr. Charmont declared himself enchanted. He is more than willing; he is eager to give her lessons. Being typically French, however, his fees (I enclose the schedule along with his evaluation of her work) are rather higher than I can squeeze out of the housekeeping money.

Your first kind letter to me said that you were mine to command at any time. I do not command, sir, I appeal.

Yours respectfully,
Caroline Ettington

AN UNFORGOTTEN LOVE

Telegraph from London, May 8th:

Much impressed by Monsieur Charmont's report. His bills may be submitted to and will be paid direct from this office.

G. L. Wheale

Cliff House
May 11, 1852

Dear Mr. Wheale,

My most heartfelt thanks for the promptitude of your telegraph, which I took to town immediately to show to Monsieur Charmont. When my dear child learned of the proposed lessons, she was made the happiest girl in all Cornwall.

Afterward I bethought myself of a small difficulty, which makes it necessary for me once again to throw myself on your mercy.

The bills you will receive from Monsieur Charmont will list Page Caroline Llanwelly as his pupil rather than Diane Victoria Page. That is the name my daughter—she also deems herself my daughter—calls herself.

You see, Mr. Wheale, all unknown to Lady Vaile—who I am afraid would be horrified—nearly five years ago I married a local man, a fisherman of St. Ives, Egan Llanwelly. He and three sons of his first marriage live here with us at Cliff House.

I would not want you to think that Lady

Vaile's money has been supporting them, for such is not the case. My husband is a proud man and a sensitive one. Though Lady Vaile all unknowingly gives him and his the roof over their heads, it is his labor that keeps the roof sound. He does all improvements, painting and repairs about the house, for which formerly I had to hire outside help. His earnings put the food on our table.

More important—to me—he has been a father to my girl, who has long felt abandoned by her own people. And let us make no bones about it; she was abandoned. Her mother has not been to see her since her own marriage; her mother-love consists of expensive presents.

My husband and his sons have given Page—as we all agreed to call her—a family and a sense of belonging, which she was sorely lacking.

Is this hopefully another case where we can rely on the spirit rather than the letter of the law?

Yours, in some concern,
Caroline E. Llanwelly

G. L. Wheale, Solicitor
May 19, 1852

My dear Mrs. Llanwelly,

The answer to the question posed in the last paragraph of your letter is yes, and yes again!

Under the law the child is Diane Victoria Page. As far as this office is concerned, she is Page Caroline Llanwelly, the daughter of a lady and of a gentleman who have our highest respect and esteem.

Please do not worry yourself unduly, dear madam. Lady Vaile need never know of this small deception. I am Miss Llanwelly's solicitor, as well as her trustee, and this comes under the heading of client confidentiality.

That is the personal side. Legally speaking, Cliff House—you are obviously not aware—belongs not to her mother but to young Page and is, therefore, under the trusteeship of this firm and the bank, not of Lady Vaile. It would be up to us, therefore, not to milady, to decide who might or might not live there during the minority of her daughter.

As far as we are concerned, Page is in custody to you and Mr. Llanwelly, so no problem exists about his residence in Cliff House.

Respectfully,
George Wheale

Baliol College
Oxford
December 3, 1853

Dear Father,

I wanted to prepare you for a call you may shortly be receiving from Mr. Conway Carter, an archeologist not too long back from an expedition to Greece. He gave a series of guest lectures at Oxford recently and was kind enough to take dinner with me and study some of the reports I have prepared these last years on my exhibits of our Grand Cavern fossils, as well as the college studies I did for Professor Eagels.

After several meetings, Mr. Carter made me an offer which is beyond what I have ever hoped to receive without many more years of study and experience.

He is heading a three-year expedition to Palestine to explore the origins and peoples of the Holy Land, hopefully to as far back as the Roman occupation and the time of the early Hebrews.

Father, he wants me to make one of the expedition, which is not only the opportunity of a lifetime for me but my every dream come true.

I have always known that the proper emptying-out of the Grand Cavern on our home property will be almost a lifetime's work. After this expedition, I would have the necessary knowledge and experience.

Mr. Carter does not propose to leave England for another nine months to a year, so that I will be graduated and able to spend one last summer at home.

I would be obliged to pay my own expenses if I am to go, since the expedition is privately and not too generously endowed. I should rather *say, to be perfectly honest, that you would have to pay.*

Sir, you offered me, when I came down from Oxford, a new riding horse, the renovation of the Dower House, left empty since Grandmother died, and lodgings in town for the Season.

My dear father, I will gladly relinquish all else for the benefit of joining the Conway expedition.

> *Your loving son,*
> *Rupert*

> *Cliff House*
> *May 4, 1854*

Dear Mr. Wheale,

Can you help me, please?

As you know, in the last month I have written twice to Lady Vaile, as usual sending both letters under cover to you. She has not answered either letter, and I considered the matter on which I wrote of no little urgency.

Is it possible that my letters have gone astray . . . or been somehow detained in your office?

> *Sincerely yours,*
> *Caroline Llanwelly*

Both letters delivered by me to subject before she left for summer in Derbyshire.

> *G. L. Wheale*

Cliff House
May 10, 1854

Dear Mr. Wheale,

   Thank you for your telegraph.
   Distasteful as it may be, I know now how I must handle the matter, since Lady Vaile chooses to ignore it.

                    Yours very truly,
                    Caroline Llanwelly

                    Cliff House
                    St. Ives, Cornwall
                    May 10, 1854

Lady Diane Vaile
Landsdowne Hall
Derbyshire

Dear Lady Vaile,

   As the mother of two daughters, I know you will understand an appeal that comes straight from my heart.
   You recall my niece Vicky? Although brought up in a Cornish fishing village, she happens to be the daughter of both a gentleman and a lady and has herself received the education and has all the accomplishments of a gentle-woman.
   Indeed, she has something more, for the French painter, Jean Pierre Charmont, who

instructed her in drawing over two successive summers, considers her talent to be little short of genius. She converses in French like a Frenchwoman and also speaks a little Italian. Her only educational lack, for want of an instrument, is in music, but she has a sweet, true singing voice.

Except that she has had no formal schooling, Vicky is completely equipped to be a superior governess—to teach drawing—even to conduct her own school one day.

She is too young for these at present—not quite sixteen—and I had thought there was time to spare. Unfortunately, there is not. A young fisherman of the village two years older than she, who has been almost her lifelong companion, quite recently has begun to see her in a new light.

I think Vicky is only slightly aware of Peter's feelings as yet . . . he is hardly aware of them himself. His father, with whom I have discussed this matter, and I, however, have both seen enough to make us uneasy. Young marriages are commonplace hereabouts, but this one would be a disaster for both. As the wife of a fisherman, Vicky would sink into a lifetime of hard work, child bearing and a stifling loss of the freedom that is the breath of life to her. There would be no time for her painting, which is her dearest occupation. Peter is a fine young man, too. He deserves better than a wife embittered by a lifetime of regrets.

You once said, dear Lady Vaile, that you longed for the opportunity to return the debt you had incurred to me. I only did my duty as your governess, but your kindness in making so much of my services has induced me to make this appeal to you.

There is a fine school in Paris which Vicky could attend for the next two years, if only she had a sponsor to help in her expenses. Monsieur Charmont feels quite certain he can secure her a partial scholarship, and there is the added advantage that she could continue her private drawing lessons with him.

There are others I might turn to who I think would be glad to help someone in Vicky's position. I thought of you first, however, because you have always maintained such an interest in her.

Forgive what may appear presumption, but it seemed only natural to make this appeal to you before I tried the other means necessary.

With my most heartfelt thanks,

Caroline Ettington

Miss Ettington, pray do not write to me at my home again; you know it would involve me in difficulties with my husband if at this late date he learned of Vicky's background, and I have told you he sees my mail first. Most fortunately, he did not read between your lines, and it is agreed between us that Vicky should have this chance. You will hear direct from him or the solicitors but don't write to me here again.

D.V.

Ecole Ferrier
Paris, France
September 8, 1854

Dearest Mama, Da, Peter, Powys and Patric,

I crossed the Channel without a moment's seasickness, and here I am—I still can't believe it—in France.

When I remember the five of you and my dear Cliff House, I could weep both with family-sickness and with homesickness and pack my portmanteaux and hurry home to you.

At such times I make myself think of my lessons ... of M. Charmont ... the art museums. I walk along the boulevards—it is such an exciting city—and I tell myself not to be foolish, this is the opportunity of a lifetime, the two years will pass quickly, busily, happily!

I love you all.

Your daughter and sister,
Page

AN UNFORGOTTEN LOVE

Jerusalem
October 10, 1854

My dear Father,

Just a brief line to let you know that after a long and arduous journey, we have finally arrived. The setting-up of our camp and employment of local workers occupies almost all our waking hours. We battle daily with incredible heat, dust, thievery, bribery and chicanery at every level of government.

Lest you think I am complaining, father, be assured I have never been happier. I derive genuine enjoyment from this bargaining we must do, and I can scarcely wait to get on with our dig. There is much to do, so much to learn.

I can never sufficiently express my gratitude to you for giving me this opportunity. My love to the girls, to Marcus, too, if he comes home on leave, and, of course, to my stepmother.

Yours affectionately,
Rupert

Cliff House
May 11, 1856

My dearest Page,

Of course, you must go to Italy at summer's end. Such an opportunity is not to be missed. To study under Antonio Grazzi, as well as to see all the fine old masters . . . you would improve your Italian immeasurably as well. I have no doubt that after two years there, you would be fit to instruct in the finest school in England. Think how much that will mean in the brochure if one day you should found your own school!

The pension arrangements mentioned by Madame Charmont sound excellent to me. I would want you adequately chaperoned, of course. I have perfect faith in your judgment, but we must think of your reputation. Dame Grundy's long tongue might reach even to England.

I have spoken to Mr. Wheale, who has been most kind in reassuring me about the financial arrangements, so these need not give you any concern.

On the personal side, Page, my loved daughter, I have ever tried to be honest with you. Just recently, after a long period of unhappiness following your departure, Peter has begun to show an interest in Maura Pengilly. Perhaps you may remember her? Tall, long-legged and carrot-haired? Also, a very sprightly, proper wife for him . . . but if you came back at this critical juncture, who knows?

Go to Italy, our Page. We will miss you greatly, as we have always missed you, but believe it is best for all concerned.

Your loving mother
Caroline Llanwelly

AN UNFORGOTTEN LOVE

Caesarea, Palestine
December 23, 1858

My dear Father,

At long last I can give you the news you may have despaired of ever hearing. I will embark some time in the middle of April and hopefully will arrive in England in the early part of the summer.

As soon as ever I set foot on land, I shall come at once to Derbyshire, so please do not await me in the heat and squalor of London, which I know is so distasteful to you.

I marvel, as I write, that when I leave, it will be closer to five years than to four since I departed England. The years here have been beyond anything great; I would not trade them for a nabob's fortune. Now that my adventure is almost over, however, I must confess that my heart beats fast at the thought of once again seeing my home, my land, and especially, my dear father, you.

Devotedly,
Rupert

April 2, 1859

Page, my dear, there's been a lot of tides gone out since last we swam together in our cove, and what I have to say is not news you'll best be happy to hear, but say it I must.

It's time you came home, lass. Happen later you can go back to foreign parts if that's the life you want, but right now Aunt Etti and our da are bad in need of you.

Eighteen months gone, da had some kind of stroke, and though he came back from it, to this day, on the left side, his face and body are kind-of stifflike, and he can't move or work the way he used to. He couldn't manage on the boat without me, but times here in Cornwall are so hard . . . the fishing's fallen off . . . and the prices, and we're feeling the famine from Ireland.

Thank God for Cliff House. Page, I know well, lass, it's your money gives us a comfortable roof over our heads, but I've Maura and my own two girls to think of now, and I've had to give serious thought to joining Powys in Australia. Seems like there's more of a future there, but how could I ever leave da?

Patric tries to help, but he's no fisherman, that's the truth. Aunt Etti filled his head so full of books, they're his whole life, and if he does what he wants, he'll be a schoolmaster, not follow the sea, and I can't say he would be wrong.

Da and Aunt Etti would have my head for washing if they knew I had written this, but now there's an added worry. Something's wrong with her eyes, Page. She doesn't say so, but we've all noticed and have the fear—I think she has it, too—that her sight may be going.

AN UNFORGOTTEN LOVE

We need you, girl, that's the God's honest truth.

Your brother,
Peter Llanwelly

Rome, Italy
April 14, 1859

Beloved family, I am on my way home to you.

Page Caroline Llanwelly

Chapter Ten

"MY DEAR MISS LLANWELLY." MR. WHEALE
smiled beamingly as he came around the corner
of his desk, right hand outstretched. Her slim,
strong fingers gripped his like any man's; they
shook hands heartily.

"How well you look, my dear; the Cornish air
must suit you."

"Indeed it does," she said in the slightly
throaty voice that had intrigued him from the
time of their first meeting nearly a year before. It
seemed always to contain—even in times of
great anxiety—a slight undercurrent of amusement, as though she were having a private
laugh at the foibles of the world.

"I never knew how much it suited me," she went on, "till I took in my first great gulps of it after five years abroad. Mother's milk never suited a baby more than those lovely fish-and-ocean breaths suited me," she wound up with the lovely gurgle of laughter so like Lady Vaile's.

Mr. Wheale was hard put to it to suppress the twitching of his own lips. No young lady of twenty-two that he had ever known dared speak of mother's milk in that casual way or would have heard it mentioned without a fiery blush.

She was an original, was Page Llanwelly, as well as a girl of extraordinary talent and resource, a tribute to the mother who had raised her rather than the one who had given her birth.

"Sit down, my dear, do," he said, urging her toward a comfortable armchair. Page disposed herself in it gracefully, then crossed her legs, exposing much more of her white stockings and ankles than the customs of the time decreed a gentlewoman should.

"How may I help you?" he asked gently, and she gave him a sudden rueful smile.

"It must seem to you I only arrive here when I want something of you," she agreed, "and I am afraid . . ." She held out her hands deprecatingly and wrinkled up her nose.

"I am one of your trustees. It is right and proper that you turn to me."

"Good. Because, dear sir, I want more money."

"Is your mother—" he began anxiously, only to be interrupted by her hasty assurance.

"Mama is well, Mr. Wheale. Indeed, she looks ten years younger than when I first returned home. The operation was a complete success. And da has made marvelous progress, too, especially since he gave up the fishing. Oh, we've done fine this past year, I promise you, but now we can't stand still. The little house Patric and I rented for our day school is fair bursting at the seams, we've outgrown it so quickly. There's a fine big house right in the center of town come onto the market. Old Lady Firth, who just died, lived in it alone these last ten years. Her nephew inherited, and he just wants to get rid of it fast. He's aware that it's not been improved or kept in good repair, and he's prepared to let me have it at a bargain."

"You want it for a school?"

"It's ideal. Da could supervise and help renovate it—it would keep him busy and happy—and he'd be the caretaker and in charge of the gardens. Mama would act as headmistress and supervise the housekeeper and cook and maids . . . even teach some classes when she felt so inclined. There's enough space for half a dozen pupils to live in, not just our day girls. We've had dozens of requests for that."

"Dear me, you seem to have done extraordinarily well."

"There's a crying need for schools like ours for

the kind of girl we cater for—daughters of the new-rich, merchants and men in trade, even farmers who, now that they have money, want to give their girls an education in a school where they won't be snubbed and made unhappy."

"I admire your enterprise more than I can say."

"Yes, but will you finance it?" she asked shrewdly. "Out of my own money, of course. And to provide a home for my parents and Patric."

"But you own Cliff House!"

"I want to make it over to Peter. He and Maura have just had their third child and first son. They need it the most, and the situation of it is too rough for mama and da now. I shall visit often, of course, but Cornwall won't be my home anymore."

"It won't?"

"Not once the school is set. I don't really have the patience for teaching, not like my mother; and if I'm to get anywhere with my painting . . . well, it's London I've set my sights on now. Before I go on with my own plans, though, I want to be able to set up the school, which will eventually be Patric's. And I want a new boat for Peter and some land money for Powys in Australia. There's all those thousands and thousands of pounds sitting around waiting till I'm twenty-five. . . . Do I really have to wait the whole three years?"

"I can let you have some of the accumulated

interest—a fair-sized sum, though I doubt it would cover quite all you mentioned—but there is no way that the principal could be touched, unless you marry before your twenty-fifth birthday."

"Well, could I get a loan against it?"

Mr. Wheale looked scandalized. "The interest would be usurious!"

"If I must, I must. I have no other way. I sold all the conscience jewels Lady Vaile presented me over the last dozen Christmases."

"My dear!"

"Did I sound bitter? I'm not, you know. But I *am* willing to get anything I can out of her for my family's good. Do you suppose—could you ask her for a loan against my legacy? I could sign a note." She grinned. "Interest-free, of course."

"I doubt . . . but there's no harm in trying. You might better approach her yourself while you are both in town."

"Lady Vaile is here in London? I thought she was always in Derbyshire at this season."

"Usually, I believe, but . . ." He snapped his fingers. "Yes, now I recollect. Her daughters—your half-sisters—need a new governess. She and Lord Vaile came to town to conduct some interviews."

Page rose from the depths of the armchair and walked to the far end of the room, looking out the window onto a dismal London street scene. When she turned back, his heart sank, for her blue eyes were ablaze with a mixture of mischief and excitement that he had learned meant, if not exactly trouble, at the very least disturbance of his peace.

"Mr. Wheale, I must go back to my hotel room and make ready. Would you please send a messenger to me just as soon as you have gotten me an interview for governess to Lady Vaile's daughters?"

"Impossible!"

"Surely not." She eyed him reproachfully. "You *are* trustee for Lady Vaile in the matter of her own inheritance as well as mine, are you not? On hearing that she was on the lookout for a governess, what could be more natural than your recommendation of a sterling candidate"— she sank down in a deep curtsey, her hands pointing inward to herself—"in the person of one Page Llanwelly?"

She then bounced upright again to remind him jauntily, "A name, I might remind you, with which she is completely unfamiliar."

"You have not the appearance that a woman would want in a governess!"

"But I shall, dear sir, I shall, by the time your messenger arrives. I am leaving for a milliner's immediately to buy myself a suitably sober bonnet. My traveling dress is black and quite *unbe*coming; it will do for the occasion."

"And your face?"

"Mama told me I don't look at all like Lady

112

Vaile, except my coloring. Never fear, I won't be recognized; she's supposed to be a beauty."

"You are still too pretty!" he snapped, goaded.

"Dear Mr. Wheale, no one who sees me at my interview will agree with you. Do send word to my hotel quickly."

She blew him a quick kiss, waved her hand and whisked out the door before he could offer any further objections.

Some five hours later, when she was ushered into the library of the house on Prince's Gate, overlooking Hyde Park, a casual observer might almost have agreed with her prediction. She looked a bit shabby in the worn black traveling dress. Not a single golden tendril had escaped from the confines of the big bun under her rather ugly gray bombazine bonnet. She had used a charcoal sketching pencil to color in the arch of her eyebrows and darken them in the mistaken belief that thick, straight brows gave her a slightly more grim and governess-y look.

The man who rose courteously from an armchair and laid down his book as she came into the room was not, however, a casual observer. He looked at her penetratingly even as he said in a somewhat doubtful manner, "Miss Llanwelly?"

She laughed, which she had not meant to do, having observed for years both in France and Italy as well as in Cornwall, the effect of that sound on susceptible men. "Llan-welly," she corrected. "The accent is on the first syllable."

She stared at him, doubtful in her turn, knowing he could not be Lord Vaile. She had a long-ago sketch of the tall, plump, balding baron in her portfolio at home. This man was too young, too well-built, too flat of stomach and wide of shoulders, as well as far too dark-faced and beetle-browed to be a Vaile at all. Good lord, he looked as though, instead of fawn trousers and a frock coat, he would be more at home in a burnoose or perhaps with a gypsy bandanna wrapped about his rather odd-colored yellow-white hair.

Their staring match continued for a full minute before she remembered why she was there.

"Sir," she asked on a note of inquiry, "will Lady Vaile be joining us?"

"No, I am sorry. Lady Vaile is feeling poorly, and Lord Vaile was unexpectedly called away on business."

He smiled pleasantly in the face of her obvious dismay. "I am fully competent to conduct the interview," he assured her, eyebrows quirked. "They trust my judgment."

At which provocative remark, she cast him a look with her blue eyes blazing in a way all too familiar to Mr. Wheale.

Her voice was dulcet enough, however, when she sat down in the chair he indicated, inquiring, "Would you wish to look at my credentials, Mr.-Mr.—?"

"Vaile. Rupert Vaile. You would—if hired—be instructing my young sisters."

How silly you are! Page scolded herself, tremblingly thankful all the same that she was no longer standing. But who could have believed even fifteen years would change the gentle boy with his light brown hair and thin, pale, clever face into this-this—

And yet, as she studied him, not with the distorted memory of a hopelessly smitten seven-year-old but with an artist's more measuring and discerning eye, she could see now the sameness of the features. His face might be older and swarthy as a gypsy's, but it was still thin and clever with an aquiline nose, full-lipped mouth and prominent chin.

The sun had browned his skin and bleached his hair. He had his father's height, if not his girth, a good figure, an assured manner, but he was—

"Miss Llanwelly?"

"I beg your pardon."

"I asked you to tell me about yourself."

"Oh yes, of course." Page made a determined effort to pull herself together. A fine way to get a position as governess, behaving like a schoolgirl herself!

"I was educated privately at home," she began, her hands folded primly in her lap.

"Later I was sent to finishing schools in France and Italy. I speak and write both languages fluently. I am competent to teach English grammar, literature, and history, world geography, mathematics, some elementary science—"

"Such as?" he interrupted.

"A little botany." He looked disappointed. "And archeology." His eyes grew bright with interest. "I think, by studying past civilizations," she went on carefully, "we have much to learn about our own."

He was studying her *now*, decided Page with sudden insight, not with a connoisseur's appreciation of an attractive woman, as Mr. Wheale had feared, but rather as though she were a particularly interesting fossil.

"Anything more?" he murmured.

"I can teach drawing." She reached into a folder and handed him some watercolors of flowers and children at play.

After a cursory glance, "Very pretty," he said dismissingly, and Page smiled in inward appreciation, glad he knew the innocuous drawings she had brought were undeserving of praise.

"I presume," she continued, "that Lady Vaile would wish me to supervise your sisters' deportment and manners. I also believe in plenty of fresh air and exercise."

"My father will want to check over your references. You were told, I believe, that you will mostly reside at Landsdowne Hall, our home in Derbyshire, rather than here in town?"

"You mean—I am hired?"

"Unless you have some objection . . . or question. The salary, by the way"—he named without hesitation the maximum sum his father had set for "a gentlewoman of superior accomplishments"—"seventy-five pounds."

Chapter Eleven

THE HOUSEMAID ASSIGNED TO SHOW HER TO HER bedroom pushed open the door of a small and stiflingly hot chamber. "This is it," she said in tones of disparagement, "for as long as you stay."

The natural arch of Page's eyebrows lifted above the lines she had pencilled in. "I take it," she inquired sweetly, "you don't expect me to stay too long?"

The maid shrugged. "They hardly ever does. Miss Eliza and Miss Emily, they're a rare handful."

Page was at the single window, trying to force it open.

"You may be right, you may be wrong, but as long as I'm here, I prefer a room with air. Please get that stiff-rumped fellow in the hallway—what's his name, Perkins—up here to open this for me, will you?"

"Mr. Perkins! Well, I never!" declared the maid, her eyes fairly bulging from their sockets. "Why, he's the butler. He wouldn't so demean himself."

"Indeed? Well, then, pray find some member of this household who would not consider the opening of a window a chore beyond his strength. Either that, or bid the housekeeper change my room."

Half an hour later the maid was back. "Here's your supper tray, miss, and Mrs. Sibley says as how you'll have to wait till tomorrow for the window when someone can speak to the estate carpenter."

Page whisked the napkin off the tray and studied the contents for ten seconds.

"What is your name?"

"Nellie, miss, but I'm just maid to the young ladies. I . . ."

"Mrs. Sibley is the housekeeper?"

"Yes, miss, but I just do what I'm told. I . . ."

"Is she in the kitchen now?"

"Yes, but . . ."

"Good. Lead the way, and don't forget the tray, Nellie."

"Mrs. Sibley?" Page was asking politely a few moments later, "I am Miss Llanwelly, the new governess. If you will examine the dinner tray just sent up to me, you will discover for yourself, I am sure, that its contents are not only unfit for human consumption but a disgrace to any housekeeper's management. The chop is burned, the potatoes are underdone, the gravy is congealed. Need I go on? In this great house, moreover, fairly overrun with servants"—she looked about at six of them—"there should be, I would think, at least *one* able-bodied man with the capacity to open a stuck window. Now I dislike very much having to complain to Lord Vaile on my first day here, but I want my window opened and a decent dinner served me within the hour or I shall have no other alternative. Nellie?"

"Yes, miss."

"Please show me back to my room. I am uncertain if I remember the way. Mrs. Sibley, good evening."

Nellie departed practically at a run, and Page sailed majestically after her.

Forty minutes later she was seated at a little table drawn up before the open window, eating from a tray heaped high with the same good foods that had graced the family table.

"Good God!" she reflected soberly. "I don't need their damn job and their stuffy little room and their damned seventy-five pounds and the leavings of their table. If I did . . ."

She thought with a shudder of the governesses who had preceded her. Perhaps penniless or alone in the world. At that moment she despised all Vailes, not just Diane, but her husband and Rupert, too, and their cruelly snobbish servants, as well as the "rare handful," her own two unknown half sisters.

How strange, she thought the next morning, to be standing in front of her blood mother as a stranger, curtseying with false respect, murmuring her name.

"Lady Vaile . . . my pleasure."

Diane Vaile was still a beauty, a faded one, but a beauty. She had to work harder at it, of course, that was obvious. Nature had never been so generous as to retain the golden glow of her hair, the creamy pink of her cheeks. Wisely, any telltale lines at her throat were covered by a mass of lacy ruffles topped by strings of pearls.

"And these are your new pupils, my daughter Eliza, going on fourteen." She waved languidly at an undeveloped miniature of herself. "And this is Emily—she's nearly twelve." Emily was slim and dark, more like a Vaile.

"Girls," she told her daughters fretfully, "your father is very determined that you take full advantage of what Miss Llanwelly has to offer."

Emily shrugged, but Eliza murmured wickedly, "Oh, yes, mama, we'll take full advantage of her."

"I hope, Miss Elizabeth," Page said as soon as Lady Vaile had exited the schoolroom, "you did not mean what I think you meant?"

"I don't know, Miss Llanwelly." Elizabeth

looked at her with great wide guileless eyes just like her own. "What did you think?"

Score one to you, sister, thought Page, even as she said aloud, "Let us understand one another, Miss Elizabeth. The only advantage you are going to take is of any knowledge I may be able to impart to you. *Capisce?*"

"Huh?"

"That's Italian. It means, do you understand? It also, in this case means, you had better understand."

Lady Vaile came tripping back, the train of her dressing gown trailing on the floor.

"I forgot to tell you. I want them to have at least an hour or two a day of the backboard. They can take some of their lessons in it, can't they? Or use it while they do their embroidery? I'm determined by the time they have their coming out they will stand up regally. I don't intend either of my daughters to be one of those great awkward slouching debutantes."

Page looked at her sullen-faced sisters after their mother trailed out again.

"Where and what is this backboard?" she asked cautiously.

"Over there near the desk, and if you think you're going to strap me into *that* two hours a day," Elizabeth said insolently, "you were never more mistaken."

Page wasn't listening. She was walking all around the backboard, studying it with wide incredulous eyes.

"What on earth is this leftover from the Spanish Inquisition doing in your schoolroom?" she inquired of both girls.

"It's for improving our posture," recited Emily, "so we'll be beautiful someday and get rich husbands."

"We tied the last governess into it, so she couldn't get out, and left her all one afternoon, that's why she left," said Eliza, smiling unexpectedly.

"Well, if she did it to you, I don't know that I blame you for returning the favor. Does your mother visit the schoolroom often?" she added thoughtfully.

"Hardly ever—after the introduction."

"Good!" said Page, without a qualm of conscience. "Then let's put this thing out of sight in a dark cupboard. It gives me the horrors just to look at it. I have something far better for your posture. Tell me," she asked, when the backboard had been disposed of, "is there a brook or stream, perhaps even a lake here at Landsdowne?"

"We have the trout stream."

Page shook her head.

"There's a pond about half a mile from the Dower House where Rupert lives."

"Your brother . . . doesn't live here?"

"No such luck, not that I blame him. He can live at the Dower House without any stupid rules. He has his meals whenever he pleases, and he reads at table. He doesn't dress a dozen times a day, just wears the same old clothes to dig in his cavern and, except when he comes to us, puts on anything at hand that's clean enough for dinner, even his dressing gown."

Conscious of a strong feeling of disappointment that Rupert lived under a different roof, which she rigorously tried to suppress, Page pursued the subject of the pond. "Is it walking distance from here?"

The girls agreed without too much enthusiasm that if the weather wasn't too hot or too humid, too windy or too wet, perhaps the distance was walkable.

"Then let us walk there this afternoon," said Page, blandly ignoring their indifference, "and I'll show you—painlessly—how to acquire straight backs."

Her disposal of the backboard had disarmed them somewhat, but they were still suspicious enough of all the breed of governesses to be far from friendly on the afternoon stroll.

As they walked along, Page named in French as well as English the different trees and flowers they came across, as well as the birds darting through the leaves and one or two small animals that dashed across the woodland path. Eliza and Emily repeated the names obediently, but she had no illusion that they were taking any pleasure in the expedition or felt any great trust of her. Not till they came to a clearing and Emily pointed. "There it is."

"Oh, this is perfect!" Page declared, clambering down onto a small raft chained to the low stone wall about the pond. She took a full jar out of the basket she had been carrying over her arm and proceeded to tie a cord around the neck. Then she lowered the jar gently into the water and tied the other end of the cord around a ring at the front of the raft.

"What on earth is that?" asked Eliza, forgetting to be formal.

"Tea. It will get nice and chilled in the water."

"Cold tea. Ugh."

"Not at all. You will find, when it's really cold, tea is a most reviving drink. You'll be glad of it later."

"Why?" asked Emily suspiciously.

"Because I think you may be tired, and there's nothing like refreshment when one is wearied," said Page cheerfully as she unlaced her boots and stripped off her stockings.

While the two girls watched her, openmouthed in shock, she pulled down her skirts and petticoats and stepped out of them, untied the bow at her neck and unbuttoned her blouse.

"Well," she asked in apparent unconcern, "which of you girls will try first or would you prefer to go together?"

Eliza and Emily both spoke at once.

"Try what?" asked Eliza.

"Go where?" demanded Emily.

"Why, into the pond for a swim," Page said

matter-of-factly, balancing on the edge of the raft for a moment before she made a straight shallow dive into the water.

She came bobbing up in seconds, declaring with enthusiasm to her sisters, "Oh, it's lovely. Aren't you longing to come in?"

Pretending to be unaware of their awestruck gaze, she swam all around the raft, then tipped over on her back, floating with her eyes closed.

"Oooh, I'd be afraid," said Emily, but Eliza was already tearing off her clothes.

Stripped down to a thin chemise and lace-edged bloomers, she sat down on the edge of the raft. "What shall I do now?" she asked.

"Hold on and lower yourself into the water . . . slowly . . . that's right . . . keep holding on. Easy . . . easy . . ."

"Just like the jar of tea," said Eliza flippantly, though her eyes looked a little wide and scared.

"Right, just like the jar of tea. Now remember one thing, you don't have to be frightened; you're as safe with me as you would be on dry land. Let's start first with your breathing . . ."

Eliza's lesson lasted half an hour. Before it had ended, she dared to take a half dozen wobbly strokes all by herself, with Page swimming alongside, bolstering her courage.

Emily's progress, when her turn came, was slower and less sure but enough to make her volubly happy.

Both girls sat on the raft, chattering excitedly,

while Page enjoyed a swim clear across the pond and back.

"Where did you learn to swim, Miss Llanwelly?"

"My brothers taught me when I was—oh, perhaps half your age."

"Did you swim in—you know, like this—in just your chemise and drawers?"

Page grinned mischievously. "As a matter of fact, until I was nearly your age and mama caught us, most of the time we wore nothing at all."

"You swam *naked* with your brothers!"

"I surely did."

"Was your mother furious? Did you get whipped?"

Page looked mildly surprised. "No, of course not. Mama just told me that once a girl starts getting breasts, she's liable to attract trouble if she bounces them around in public." She laughed reminiscently. "Someone must have said something to the boys, too, because round about the same time, they took to wearing their underdrawers."

"You must have a very strange family."

"Oh, I do," said Page softly. "Very strange, indeed. Eliza, why don't you bring up the jar of tea? Emily, you spread out these napkins. And . . . good, here are the sponge cakes, a little bit crumbly but edible."

"However did you get them from Cook?"

"I conveyed my orders to the kitchen by Mr. Perkins," Page informed them grandly. "When I take you two on an educational project, I told them, Lord Vaile will be extremely displeased if the staff does not give me full cooperation. This"—she waved her arm toward the pond and commenced pouring the tea into three small glasses—"is an educational project."

Eliza and Emily collapsed in helpless giggles, and before too long Page joined in. When they all quieted down the girls sipped warily at their tea.

"Goodness gracious, it's good!"

"Of course. Didn't I say so? After all, I'm the governess. I *ought* to know."

"You," said Eliza with deep conviction, "are not like any other governess we ever had."

"Miss Llanwelly, can we go swimming tomorrow again? Can we go swimming every day?" Emily begged.

"Well, that depends. There's a little matter of French, composition and history to say nothing of mathematics and literature. I would think . . . well, let me put it this way . . . if the morning classes go well, then lessons in swimming can follow every fine afternoon."

"That sounds like bribery," giggled Emily, "which father disapproves of."

"Bribery, stuff!" Eliza gave an unladylike snort. "It sounds like the blackmail I read about in Nellie's police magazine."

"Bribery and blackmail!" cried Page, as though much struck by this novel notion. "You

know, girls"—she smiled at them benignly—
"you may be right. What are you going to do
about it?"

There was a short silence, then Emily dribbled
some crumbs of sponge cake down her throat.
"Mathematics and literature, I think," she said
resignedly.

Eliza closed her eyes. "French, composition
and history," she said and shrugged.

Chapter Twelve

RUPERT VAILE STRODE ALONG THE BACK ROAD leading to the Dower House, his mind churning with excitement, his two hands cupped against his chest, holding and at the same time shielding the tiny almost-perfect skull they held. It was the finest fossil specimen he had ever uncovered on the cavern floor. Too stirred up to go on digging, he had stopped work a good hour earlier than usual to take it back to his laboratory.

As he was passing by the pond he heard his sisters' voices, high and shrill and unexpectedly happy. Then he heard the laugh, which he recognized at once. It had haunted him strangely since he interviewed the governess in London. It was not the usual artificial, feminine titter that was such an assault on the ears but a full-bodied, full-throated, almost suggestive sound.

Flushing slightly at his thoughts, he said aloud derisively, "Suggestive of what, my fine boy-o?" Long hours of working alone had taught him both to ask and to answer his own questions. This one was suddenly answered for him.

Still cradling the skull protectively, he used an elbow to push aside a screening bush, giving himself a full-length view of the pond. His sisters were scrambling out of it onto the raft, their undergarments clinging to their figures in a way that would undoubtedly have caused his stepmother to shriek or to swoon.

Unnecessary, he decided, in the case of Emily, who was as flat and straight in front as she was in back. Eliza, on the other hand, showed the budding figure of the woman she would become.

Not at all proper, their state of dress or undress. On the other hand, their faces looked animated and alive instead of set in their usual sullen masks. No one but he ever passed this way, so where was the harm?

He shrugged, prepared to walk on, just as a third figure, the unforgettable Miss Llanwelly, emerged from the water. She, too, wore only the briefest of cotton undergarments, and for all the cover they gave her, she might have been wearing nothing at all.

In his bemusement, he lowered his elbow and the bush slapped back against his face. Rupert almost dropped the cherished skull.

He no longer needed to ask what her laugh had been suggestive of. It was a perfect match for the lush body standing on the raft. She was long-legged as a ballerina, with sturdy calves, shapely ankles and slender pointing feet. The gown she had worn at her interview gave no hint of the sloping shoulders, the rounded hips and, above all, the firm, fantastically full breasts pushing against the clinging wet cotton of her chemise.

Her hair, which he had not been able to see under her rather ugly bonnet, was a golden wheat color, oddly like Eliza's. It now hung over her shoulders and down her back in masses of dripping ringlets.

She was standing in profile so he could not see her from the rear, but in that moment he would have recklessly wagered his precious fossil that those hips could not possibly curve into a flat, skinny bottom. A backside that matched the rest of her would be . . .

As he looked down and noticed the curling motion of his fingers, his hands tightening about the skull as they were yearning to do about something of much more flesh and substance, he barely restrained a shout of laughter.

At that moment her own inimitable laugh rang out again; she turned and bent over to reach into a basket. He was shaken to the core by the indisputable proof presented that nature had indeed endowed her as generously behind as it had before.

The three sat down together on the dock; they appeared to be eating from the basket. Rupert released his elbow, allowing the bush to spring into place. The excitement bubbling up in him as he plodded on to the Dower House no longer centered around the dead past or the small pathetic reminder of it that he was carrying. All his thoughts and emotions were centered on one lovely, laughing, very-much-alive young woman.

While he was washing the skull in his own special solution, the indigent Irishman hired in Palestine two years before as a man-of-all-work came hurrying into the laboratory to exclaim over the newest specimen. Servants' gossip had quickly spread word of it throughout the house.

"Yes," said Rupert almost absentmindedly, busy now with his labeling. "It's the most promising fossil I have found here yet. Sean, see to laying out my clothes, will you. . . ." He looked down at his hands. "And a bath? As soon as I'm finished with this, I'm going over to the Hall. Better tell Mrs. Pearley I won't be here for dinner."

Two hours later he was sitting in the library

with his father, sampling a new Madeira and wondering how to introduce the subject most on his mind.

"Glad to see your nose out of your bones, my boy," Lord Vaile had greeted his heir expansively, flipping his braid-trimmed tailcoat up as he sat down. He cast a quick eye over Rupert's plain waistcoat and dark frock coat. "Glad to see you out of those odd cotton trousers, too, lord knows. Sir Angus mistook you for the gardener the other day when he rode by with me." He laughed heartily as he handed over a glass of wine. "I didn't enlighten him. What do you think, Rupert? A good buy?"

Rupert lowered his head over the glass held between his hands, then took an experimental taste, rolling the wine about his mouth. He swallowed slowly.

"Impeccable, sir." He smiled across at his father. "Your judgment is never at fault."

"Pooh, nonsense." But Lord Vaile's face was ruddy with pleasure.

"Speaking of judging new quantities—are you satisfied with the governess I chose, father? I have been a little concerned since I decided on her over the one you had been leaning toward."

"Your stepmother is pleased with her, and she appears to deal well with Eliza and Emily. They seem more settled, I think. I had meant to have her join us for Sunday dinner and perhaps talk to her privately here afterward."

Rupert nodded approvingly. "Yes, the woman

who supervises my sisters' manners should be seen in a family setting," he agreed with only the slightest twinge of conscience for his own duplicity. "But then, why wait for Sunday?" he asked casually.

To his delight, his father needed no further pressing. The bell was rung immediately and Perkins instructed, "My compliments to Miss Llanwelly; I would be pleased if she would join us at the supper table. And please inform Lady Vaile."

Having been privileged to watch her from behind a bush, wearing next to nothing, the heir did not share in Lord and Lady Vaile's surprise when Miss Llanwelly entered the parlor at Landsdowne Hall, a Vaile sister on either side of her.

She might have been a visiting gentlewoman or a member of the family. Her gown was of primrose yellow satin with an attached ruffled cape of Devonshire cream chiffon. Her only jewelry was a simple gold locket on a black velvet ribbon about her throat. It hung just above the modestly cut but fitted decolletage, in no way distracting from the suggestion of hidden splendor.

Eliza and Emily curtseyed prettily, Page inclined her head. The gentlemen rose to their feet and Lady Vaile sat, looking slightly aggrieved. The governess was not supposed to look so—so—

Her mind would not even allow her to supply the missing word but wandered off on a new tack. Nor did one expect to see the governess wearing what could almost be mistaken for a Paris gown.

"Your dressmaker must be very skilled, Miss Llanwelly," she said at the first opportunity. "Your gown could pass for Parisian."

"You have a very good eye, Lady Vaile," Page said composedly. "It is from Paris. A birthday gift before I left France two years ago."

Across the dinner table she met Rupert's frankly amused eyes, and quite suddenly her heart turned over and her appetite fled. She had to force down a few mouthfuls of the turtle soup, and she felt a sick qualm at the very sight of a hefty slice from the saddle of mutton put upon her plate.

Oh God! she thought in panic. I'm not seven years old anymore, and he's not thirteen. He'll be Lord Vaile one day even if, unlike most gentlemen, he spends his time usefully mucking about in a cavern. I mustn't forget that I am the governess here—*just* for a time and *just* for a purpose.

At dinner's end Lord Vaile rose along with his wife, explaining that he and Rupert would take their wine in the library and join her presently in the drawing room.

"Miss Llanwelly, if you would be so obliging, might I see you in the library in a quarter of an hour?"

"Certainly, my lord."

She followed Lady Vaile and her daughters

and spent the intervening time listening to Eliza torture the strings of a huge golden harp. When the chimes of the clock brought her release, she hastily excused herself. The author of the torment bestowed an unsmiling wink on her as she fled the room.

Lord Vaile greeted her courteously in the library, and his son pushed forward a chair.

"Your name is quite unusual, Miss Llanwelly, at least in Derbyshire," her employer began courteously. "Welsh, I believe?"

"I believe so, sir, though I am not quite certain, my father's family having been so long in Cornwall."

"Cornwall!" She noticed that both men looked at her with quickened interest. "We used to have some family living near St. Ives."

"My da"—she fell into the vernacular deliberately as she lied—"is a Truro man."

"Your education is remarkable for . . ."

Lord Vaile hesitated out of delicacy and Page obligingly helped him out.

"My mother was a lady before her father lost his money," she said with such gentle irony that Lord Vaile failed to understand her implication. His son, however, did not and gave her a very straight look, which she unflinchingly returned.

"Lady Newhaven—perhaps you know her?" She continued her fairy tale. "She befriended me and saw to my education at home and later sent me to a language school in France, where I also taught. Her solicitor, Mr. Wheale, told me about the position available with your daughters, my lord, which fortuitously came just as I was seeking employment in England."

Lord Vaile cleared his throat. "My daughters, I must acknowledge, have been rather hard on governesses in the past. It has surprised me pleasantly that they appear so taken with you, Miss Llanwelly. Not," he added hastily, "that I believe young girls should have a say in appointing their mentors, but there is no denying your situation here will be easier if . . ."

"If I don't have to stuff education down their throats. I am fully of the same mind, my lord."

"Nevertheless, if you run into any difficulties —if they are too unruly or you think need discipline, please don't hesitate to call on me."

"Thank you very much, my lord. I hope it won't be necessary. I would think poorly of myself if I could not manage two such young girls. If they *are* a little difficult at times, it's because they are both quick and bright. The perfect pupil must necessarily be a dull one, which I would not find at all challenging. As for discipline—I never did believe that knowledge could be imparted with a rod."

He smiled faintly. "The last governess was of the opinion it could be imparted to my daughters no other way."

"Hopefully, sir, that's why she is gone and I am here."

She curtseyed when he smiled again, this time

in satisfied dismissal. Rupert accompanied her to the door, ostensibly to open it for her.

"Miss Llanwelly," he said very softly, "my father can be somewhat pompous, as I have seen you observe. He is also a very kind man and an exceptionally good one. I would not like to think you were making a May game of him along with the rest of us."

"You need not worry, Mr. Vaile," she told him even more softly. "I promise you that *your father* has my very great respect."

As she dipped down in another brief curtsey and walked away, his brows came together in a puzzled frown. He did not think she was fully aware of how strongly she had emphasized the words *your father*.

Who among them was it she did not respect? Perhaps even disliked?

He experienced a pang of dismay almost as disconcerting as it was alarming. To admire her beautiful body from behind a bush—desire it even—would be understandable in any man. But for the heir to Baron Vaile to be overly concerned with what went on inside the governess's heart and head—therein lay trouble.

Chapter Thirteen

Dear Mama,

Your letter sounded happy and cheerful, but reading between the lines, I know that you are worried. Please, please, dearest of mothers, do not be.

I know that I have already stayed here much longer than I said I would, but there has been an unexpected complication. No, mama, not the one you fear. I am talking about Eliza and Emily. They were strangers to me; they have been strangers all their lives. I did not expect to have any strong feelings for them, and to find myself regarding them as my little sisters was something unforseen. It makes me very happy that I have been—so I immodestly believe—of enormous difference in their lives. No one knows better than you that she does not know how to be a mother. Nannies, nurses, governesses, servants. . . . In the midst of an army of them, the poor dears have been utterly neglected.

Lord Vaile, I do believe, has the best of intentions, but until quite recently a half hour to an hour a day, when they were brought to the drawing room dressed up as though for guests, was the maximum amount their parents spent with them. How can anyone be a parent in one assigned hour a day of stilted conversation? When I think of you and da and the boys and all the wonderful times we had together. . . .

For my sins, now that I am so in favor, I take my meals with the family, except those that include distinguished company. Over breakfast Lord Vaile reads his paper and all the mail before passing on each letter to its rightful owner. Not mine, of course. I (I thank God) am the governess; only females in the family are subject to his moral censorship. I am sure he never regards what he is doing in that light. His father did it and his father before him, so it is taken for granted that the head of the house should be the first to open the cherished invitation Eliza has been waiting to receive for Miss Littleton's birthday party or examine the note and book sent from London by Emily's godmother before they are given to her. His own wife's letters, too!

"I think your friend Mrs. Worth a little too free and warm in her speech!" he told Lady Vaile in tones of marked disapproval just the other day, having carefully perused a letter from one of her friends in London. She actually began making weak apologies for this Mrs. Worth while he handed over her letter with obvious reluctance. If I could feel sorry for her, I would have felt sorry then. No wonder you could never write to her here unless you wanted him to read the letter!

Dinners are no less agonizing. Lord Vaile delivers a monologue on whatever politician is currently enraging him and dictates what tomorrow's weather will be; Lady Vaile discusses the gown she wore last night, the gown she will wear tomorrow, and the gowns worn by other ladies in the neighborhood.

Eliza and Emily sit silent and dull—which they are not—with their heads downcast, their hands clasped in their laps between courses. Their mother talks about them but never to them. Until their coming out, they are not quite people. Occasionally, their father—he wants to be their friend, poor man, and it is painful to watch him make the sorry attempt—throws them a conversational bone.

"And what are you studying now, hey?" he will boom across the table in a voice that could startle some of Rupert's bones into life.

"Shakespeare, Papa," Eliza will respond, like a puppet on a string. "We have started with Julius Caesar."

"Shakespeare, hey? Good. Fine. Shakespeare is a part of every proper English education."

Having finished this engrossing exchange with Eliza, it is Emily's turn. "And you, miss, are you studying Shakespeare, too?"

Emily looks up from her plate. "Miss Llanwelly is teaching me about the Roman occupation of Britain, papa."

"Excellent. Excellent." He looks down at his own plate; and then it is my turn. "A very sound curriculum, Miss Llanwelly," he tells me gravely.

Oh dear, truly I do not mean to make sport of him. He is a man of many sterling qualities, but, oh the life his women lead is sterile! I cannot leave my sisters to it yet, not until they are somewhat better equipped to handle the next governess without having to resort to tying her into a backboard! If I could but handpick the right one for them, I would leave tomorrow, even though Patric assures me that, with the new assistant, he is able to go on quite well without me!

It is true, mama, I would leave. Yes, in spite of Rupert. There—I have said it. You wanted me to, did you not? I am too wise, I hope, to try to fool you who know me only too well. I do—much against my will—have strong feelings for him. Is it really possible, do you think, to fall in love at seven years of age and never again fall out? I have often seen a special smiling look of tenderness in his eyes when he looks at me which leads me to believe that he, perhaps, has certain feelings for me, too. If he does, he says nothing, nor do I. In his eyes, I am the governess and he is a Vaile, and never the twain shall meet. In mine, the twain cannot meet for far different reasons than blueblooded snobbery. I could never lead the stultifying life of a Lady Vaile. (Not that the position is likely to be offered.)

So I shall stay with the Vailes only until I think my sisters can go on well without me and I have gotten the money I need from my lady. Then it's off to London—by the by, we go there next week for the winter—where I shall not be a gentlewoman but a painter.

Never fret, dear mama, do I not always, like the kitchen cat, land safely on my feet?

My love to da, the boys and Maura. Kiss the children and tell them I have sent them some treats from our trip to Matlock.

> Your loving daughter,
> Page

P.S. Lord Vaile's second son Marcus will be living with us at the London house. He was formerly in the army but after being wounded

*in the Crimea, resigned his commission. With
Lord Vaile's assistance, he seeks to advance in
politics or diplomacy and is presently secre-
tary to the very political Lord Bramwich. Nellie
tells me that he has the reputation of being
quite a ladies' man. Lock your door in London,
she warned me most impressively, by which I
gather the governess is considered fair prey. I
laughed and thanked her, without bothering to
tell her that my brother Peter, bless him,
taught me a trick or two worth any locked door!*

Marcus Vaile had his older brother Rupert's
height and build, but in every other way
he was utterly unlike Rupert, being as fair-
complexioned and fresh-faced as the other was
dark from the sun and bearded, as charming
and open as Rupert was contained.

He had an insatiable appetite for women
and was unable to believe—not without some
justification—that women did not have an
equally insatiable appetite for him. He was completely democratic in his tastes and would as
soon make love to a chambermaid as to a duch-
ess.

His eyes lit up with pleased anticipation when
he was introduced to his sisters' newest governess. Even Marcus would not have bedded her
predecessor, the late unlamented Miss Smythe.

He was no whit dismayed at the dinner table
that Page responded to his hand against her
thigh by a swift painful kick at his ankle. When

his hand ventured back during the next course, even as he engaged her in conversation, she continued cutting her *fricandeau* of veal and, at the same time, stomped hard on his nearest foot.

Rupert, seated across the table, saw the fleeting spasm of pain on his brother's face and frowned a little.

When the ladies had retired and the gentlemen were left to their wine, he exchanged his seat to say softly, *"Not* in our father's house and *not* our sisters' governess, Mark."

"Stick to your fossils, Rupert," Marcus advised him laughingly. "I prefer something with flesh on the bones."

"I would be reluctant to complain to our father . . ."

Marcus stared at him in astonishment. "Be damned, you have an interest there yourself!" He laughed aloud. "Let the best man win her, brother."

It never even occurred to Marcus that she could not be won; he assumed her response to his opening gambits had just been part of the game. His brother's interest lent added spice to the chase. To do him justice, he could not conceive that Rupert wanted anything more or less of Miss Page Llanwelly than he did.

Much later that night as Page sat at the small table that served her as a writing desk, preparing the next day's lessons, the door to her bedroom slowly opened. She was not at all surprised to see a suavely smiling Marcus close the door behind him.

To Marcus's disappointment, the dashing governess was still garbed in the black-and-white striped gown in which she had dined. It was buttoned high to the throat in front and the sleeves buttoned halfway up her arms.

Now he would have to engage in a battle of the buttons (to say nothing of drawstrings, petticoats and those damned whalebone corsets) as well as the inevitable battle of the sexes before she coyly succumbed to what they both wanted!

His first—and last—agreeable surprise when she stood up and he drew her into his confident embrace was the instant knowledge that she wore no corsets. So the sly little witch had been waiting for him, after all. He laughed triumphantly.

"You were expecting me, my sweet?" he asked softly.

"Not expecting," she returned easily. "Let us rather say, I anticipated that you might make the attempt."

With a swooping motion, he brought his head down, and his mouth fastened on hers in a kiss calculated to demonstrate that he was carried away by passion.

Page bore the scorching clamp of his lips with equanimity, having experienced enough French and Italian kisses not to be repelled—even if she could not be pleased—by such unshared emotion.

When he looked up, somewhat surprised that she was not melting more readily into his embrace, she stepped back and asked composedly, "I surmise that it would do no good to tell you I do not want you here, not tonight, not tomorrow, not any time?"

"Oh, my dear!" he said in laughing protest. "Why must we play these games?" He reached out toward the row of bodice buttons. "Would you not be more comfortable without the weight of your garments?"

"I would not," Page responded, shrugging, "but I can see that you won't believe me."

He dropped a light kiss on her hair; then his tongue charted a teasing trail across her forehead. "Not for a minute, my dear Miss Llanwelly, so save your breath to heat our kisses," he said, misquoting the old proverb quite outrageously.

One arm was around her again, the other struggling with the row of velvet-covered buttons. "Undo your sleeves," he whispered, and though he felt the motion of Page's body turning in his arms, he could not see the vicious upward thrust of her bent knee.

One moment he was joyfully anticipating a quick conquest and an ardent but even quicker tumble on her bed. The next second he was on the floor, doubled up with pain, moaning over and over, "Oh, Jesus, oh you bitch!"

Page closed the door quietly and hurried down

from her third-floor room. At the second-floor hallway she hesitated a moment, then summoned a passing footman with the crook of her finger.

"Would you please send Mr. Rupert Vaile's man to me."

"Very good, miss."

She waited in the hallway until Sean appeared and the footman was out of sight, then she steered him toward the stairs. "Sean, would you come upstairs with me, please? Mr. Marcus Vaile is there and in need of assistance. Quickly, please, before anyone sees us."

Inside her room, a groaning Marcus had struggled up to his knees but was having ill success in rising to his feet. Sean, taking in the situation at a glance, hurried, pokerfaced, to aid him.

Five minutes after they left together, the rake leaning heavily on his brother's man and groaning afresh with every step he took, there was a soft knock on the door. Rupert Vaile stood there when Page opened it. He looked breathless and harried.

"Ah, Sean informed you, I see. Have you been with the patient? Does he need a doctor?"

"Sean is applying some herbal remedy he picked up in the Holy Land."

"How wise of you"—Page made no effort to hide her amusement—"to keep it in the family."

She could see his swarthy face redden above the beard and added placatingly, "Cold packs are extremely efficacious, though rather painful, but you could always give him some laudanum."

"Laudanum, hell! He deserves to suffer the pain, the young swine. Page—Miss Llanwelly, I can't tell you how much I regret—how ashamed—" He was sweating profusely. "My father will be deeply mortified to know such insult has been offered to a gentlewoman under his roof."

"I sent for Sean as a means of reaching you," Page explained gently. "I don't wish your father to be told. Oh, not for your brother's sake," she rushed on before he could interrupt her, "but precisely to spare Lord Vaile the mortification you just spoke of. You see, I do, as I once told you, have the greatest respect for your father."

Rupert Vaile stared across at her with that same special smiling look of tenderness in his eyes that she had mentioned to her mother.

"You are more than generous," he told her huskily. "Thank you, I would be glad to spare him."

"Good night, Mr. Vaile."

"Good night, my—my dear Miss Llanwelly."

Chapter Fourteen

RUPERT ENTERED THE BREAKFAST PARLOR A FEW
minutes after the others were seated. "My lady,
father, your pardon. I was with Marcus. He asks
to be excused as he is somewhat fevered."

Lord Vaile looked up in concern. "Not his old
wound."

"No, father," Rupert reassured him, "just a
mild touch of the influenza, I think."

"Shall I send for Dr. Seaton?"

"I think not, sir," Rupert answered casually
from the sideboard, where he had just added a
slice of ham to his plate of scrambled eggs.
"Sean is attending him, and he—I have reason

to know from our time together in Palestine—i
an excellent sick-nurse."

Lord Vaile nodded in relief. "I will go up t
him after breakfast."

Rupert's eyes met Page's across the table
"Marcus begs that you will not, sir," he an
swered quickly. "He does not want to sprea
contagion through the house. Besides"—he ut
tered a rueful laugh—"I am afraid he is no
feeling at all sociable."

"Rupert is right, Oliver," Lady Vaile put i
quickly. "We must think of the girls."

While their parents turned toward Eliza an
Emily, who looked properly demure at this unex
pected attention, Rupert exchanged anothe
lightning glance with Miss Page Llanwelly.

In the look he directed at her was more tha
the smiling tenderness to which Page had be
come accustomed. The message of love was s
unmistakable that her usual poise was shattere
into pieces. Her eggs and coffee grew cold as sh
hid her shaking hands under her table napkin.

My God, thought Page, *he's forgetting tha
I'm the governess!*

Presently, without daring to meet his eye
again, she threw her napkin onto the table.

"Eliza. Emily. Time for lessons."

They all made their curtseys and filed out.

The lessons went very badly that mornin
with the governess, not the pupils, unable to pay
proper attention. After an hour she gave up and
flung down her pen on the desk.

"I think we all need a change. Would you like to go to an exhibition of art? I was planning to visit it on my day off, but perhaps we can make it an educational project this afternoon."

The two girls laughed heartily. Ever since their first swim, the phrase "educational project" had become their favorite joke, never staled by repetition.

"Ask papa, not mama," Eliza advised wisely. "If you say something is educational, it usually wins him over."

"You better hurry up then," Emily suggested, "he'll be leaving for his club any minute."

Acting on the extreme good sense of this advice, Page hurried down to Lord Vaile's study to make her request, only to find that he had already left for an early session of the Lords and his older son was occupying the study.

Much discomfited to find herself alone with Rupert Vaile, Page backed toward the door, muttering excuses.

"Please don't go," he said softly, advancing toward her. "I have not yet told you how very much obliged I am to you for your great consideration last night and how sorry I am that you should have been exposed to such an unpleasant experience."

"Yes, you did. There is *no* obligation, and I never was—I mean, it wasn't *that* unpleasant—I mean," she said breathlessly, her back against the door, "I never was afraid that I couldn't take care of myself."

Rupert's laugh rang out, hearty and apprecia
tive. "I know very well that you can, Miss Page
Llanwelly. I would like to know just where you
learned such efficient self-protection."

"I have three brothers, sir." A touch of arro
gance crept into her voice. "Any one of them
could break a coxcomb like Mr. Marcus in two
without half trying. They long ago taught me all
I need to know for warding off unwelcome atten
tions."

"You have more than convinced me," Rupert
told her, coming several steps closer so that his
trousers brushed against her skirt and their
bodies almost touched. There was no way in the
world she could avoid his compelling gaze, ex
cept by looking down like a bashful student
standing before her schoolmaster. This she was
proudly determined not to do. "Miss Llanwelly,"
he asked her, teasingly tender, "have you any
notion just how lovely you are?"

"Of course, I do," said Page with assumed
composure.

He grinned. "Or how impudent, my dear
Page?"

She opened her mouth, and immediately his
hand closed over it. "Hush!" he admonished her
kindly. "I know you were about to say that you
are *not* my dear Page, but you are, my love, you
are, or very soon you will be."

Then his mouth came down on hers in a kiss
utterly unlike his brother's the night before,
though it was hours later before Page would

marvel at the difference. His lips pressed lightly, sweetly, while he cradled her to him. Only after she had moved closer into the secure harbor of his arms and was standing on tiptoe, her mouth making a mute demand against his own, did the kiss become so all-encompassing that she was lost in a world of rapture. When he finally, ever so slowly, ever so gently, put her away from him, she was left with a tightened throat, quickened breath and quivering thighs.

"You must know how much I wanted to do that," Rupert told her in a far from steady voice, "by what I risked."

"R-r-risked?" Page quavered uncertainly.

"My brother is—er—out of commission for the next day or two," he said gravely, "so as well as what you told me, I have the evidence of my own eyes that you can protect yourself fiercely from unwelcome attention."

"Your . . . what you did . . . it was not unwelcome." Her voice was low, but her eyes met his without wavering.

He laughed aloud exultantly even as he caught both her hands and clipped them together over his fast-beating heart. "Do you know, my love, almost no other woman in the world would have answered as you just did? There would have been protestations about having been taken by surprise or being overpowered by my strength or some such nonsense. It's one of the things I love most about you. Your fearless, unflinching honesty."

Recollection of all the lies she had told since entering Lord Vaile's household caused a violent blush to overspread her face. "I m-must get b-back to your s-sisters," Page stammered. "They are waiting in the-the schoolroom."

"Why did you want my father, my dear?"

"Oh, yes, yes. I just wanted—well, his permission to take Eliza and Emily to an exhibition of artwork by Paolo Lorenzo. I have a card of invitation for myself and guests. But it's too late now, I suppose, perhaps another day."

"I'll hire a brougham and take you. Can you and the girls be ready in half an hour?"

"In twenty minutes," said Page, "if you'll just let me out the door."

He laughed again as he moved back from her. "I will meet you in the front hallway."

They were waiting for him in their bonnets and hoods, his two sisters dancing about with excitement, Page trying to appear properly sedate.

"Where is the exhibition?" he asked as they all went down the front steps to the waiting carriage.

"The Devane Gallery." Page handed him a slip of paper. "Here is the direction."

"Who is Paolo Lorenzo?" he pursued when they were on their way.

"He only established himself in England a few years ago. My ma—friends in Italy told me he might one day be considered one of the greatest artists of our time."

A few minutes after she entered the gallery, Page experienced a qualm of uncertainty. There were a number of impressive seascapes, a group of colorful and lively Italian street scenes, but Lorenzo's chief work consisted of ladies lying on lounges, either scantily clad or nude. His women were Rubensian in size and flesh tones, but their provocative smiles and stances, their look of bawdy good humor were pure Hogarth.

Rupert Vaile might well object to his young sisters' presence at such an exhibit, but Page, stealing a side glance at him, noted with relief that he seemed unperturbed. His years in the Middle East had no doubt somewhat cracked the straight-laced veneer that seemed to encase most Englishmen.

Emily looked around her critically, then pointed with one finger. "I like that ocean one, but those naked ladies are ugly, aren't they, Miss Llanwelly?" she asked quite audibly.

"It's rude to point, dear," Miss Llanwelly gently reprimanded her pupil, but the "unflinchingly honest" Page who had enchanted her brother, added, "No, as a matter of fact, I think the nude ladies are splendid."

Emily was not even listening; she had spied a table laid out with cakes and tea, and her mute entreaty and Page's answering nod sent her on her way.

"Emily doesn't know what she's talking about!" Eliza sputtered indignantly. "You're right, Miss Llanwelly, they're *absolutely* splendid. Look at the colors; that arm over there looks like skin I could touch. And see the hair on this one." She tugged at her governess's sleeve. "Doesn't it seem as though you could give it a good pull and that sly little smile would turn into a yell?"

Her brother was looking down at her in great astonishment. Her governess told her quietly, "That's very perceptive of you, Eliza."

"What's perceptive?"

"It means," Rupert said quietly, "that you see very clearly things that other people do not."

"Oh." Eliza shrugged. "I don't know about that. I just know"—as they all walked away she looked longingly back at the lady with the pullable hair—"I would give anything to paint like him."

"Do you paint, Eliza? But you weren't interested when I mentioned drawing lessons. You—"

"I *hate* drawing lessons!" Eliza declared with passion. "Painting silly flowers in silly vases, and the teacher telling me how I ought to see them. How can anyone tell *me*," she demanded hotly, "how *I* see something?"

"A proper drawing master would never do that," Page assured her eagerly. "Mine didn't, and I studied with Jean Pierre Charmont in France and Antonio Grazzi in Italy. Shall we try tomorrow, and if you're not happy after a few days, I could speak to your father about getting you other instruction?"

"Mama would say no," Eliza said, the old sullen mask not seen in a long time shuttering all emotion from her face. "She doesn't like me to draw, I don't know why. Once, when she asked me what I wanted for my birthday and I said, paints, she went into one of her real tizzies and said, good lord, no, one bluestocking was enough, and she made papa buy me the harp instead, and I hate the harp! I don't know who she meant either," she wound up bitterly, "unless it was Rupert. She's always making fun of his fossils; she calls them dead bones. But none of my stockings are blue, and men don't wear them, and anyway, what difference would it make?" she asked Page in an aggrieved voice, not noticing, as Rupert did, that her governess's face had gone chalk-white.

"Page—Miss Llanwelly, are you feeling faint?"

"Only with hunger." Page managed a shaky smile. "Perhaps we could join Emily at the tea table."

"I'm not hungry."

They both stared at Eliza in surprise. There was never a time when she could not eat.

"I'll look around a little more for a while. I wish," Eliza added wistfully, "I had a piece of paper and a pencil."

"Why?"

"I want to copy that one." This time Page did not trouble to correct the pointing finger but instead fished around in her large purse and came up with a small sketch pad and two drawing pencils.

"Do you think you can?"

"I don't know, but my fingers . . ." She cast a slightly apprehensive glance at her brother, then risked a vulgar confidence to the governess. "I just *itch* to try, Miss Llanwelly."

Page touched Rupert's sleeve lightly. "Let's leave her alone for a while."

He nodded and drew her arm through his, looking back at his little sister as they walked away. "I had no idea she cared so much about drawing."

"Why would you?" asked Page quietly. "You don't know her very well, after all. You are almost a generation older than the girls; you lived away from them so many years, first at school, then on your travels. Even when you came home, there was not much difference; you have your own house, and she and Emily are kept in such seclusion. Think about how seldom you spend any time with them . . . an occasional meal . . . church . . . a horse or carriage ride now and then. How many outings like this have you had with your sisters?"

"I took them to the cavern once," said Rupert slowly, "but their mother made such a fuss about the filthy condition they came home in that I . . ." His voice drifted off, then grew firm again. "No, I have no right to excuse myself so easily. They took time and trouble and interfered with my work. Emily dug too hard and broke a flint tool that was the week's best find. I was annoyed and impatient and just as glad for a reason not to be bothered with them."

Page melted at the deep trouble on his face, the rough concern in his voice.

"It's not too late," she reminded him softly, "and you can start by helping Eliza."

"How?"

"Your father places great reliance on your judgment. You could speak to him . . . stop the music lessons. Believe me, I have never heard greater punishment given to a musical instrument than she inflicts on that hapless harp. I can start the drawing lessons . . . later, perhaps, if she shows skill, she could have a London master. Lord Vaile could reassure your mother—"

"Stepmother."

"Your stepmother"—she accepted his swift correction with inward delight—"that drawing will not make a bluestocking of Eliza or," she added sardonically, "impair her ability to net a husband."

"I think you may be right. It did not impair yours."

"S-s-sir?" she stammered, stopping short in front of one of the vivid street scenes.

He pretended to study the painting with her. "You said that you had studied painting with masters in both France and Italy."

Page gasped. She had forgotten that slip of the tongue. How could she have been so stupidly forgetful as to drop that strong clue to her true identity!

"Just casually, as part of the school curriculum," she lied carelessly.

"I was merely pointing out," he explained patiently, "that, however casual, your drawing did not impair your ability to net a husband."

Page looked up at him, troubled and confused. "Mr. Vaile," she began.

"My name," he said, "to the few I love is Rupert, and I love *you*, Page, very much. I would like to be your husband if you will have me."

Page looked up at him, her heart swelling into a great ball that seemed to fill her chest to the point of bursting.

There was no time to say *yes* or *no*, or even the conventional, *this is so sudden, I need time to consider;* not even the *un*conventional, *good God, I never dreamed you meant marriage*, which was on the tip of Page's tongue.

There was only time for an exchange of glowing looks, which spoke of love, if not of marriage, as Eliza thrust the sketch pad between them.

"Look! What do you think? Did I get it right? Are her shoulders too big? I think maybe the legs aren't so good."

Page studied the sketch for several minutes. "You did well, Eliza," she said, and the pride that filled her was that of a sister, not a mere governess. "You'll do even better after lessons."

As her pupil danced ahead of them to the tea table, Page held out the sketch pad to Eliza's brother.

"Well?" she said. "Are you convinced? She has real talent, you know, not just skill. Will you speak to your father?"

"Certainly," said Rupert. "I am willing to do so even before I speak to *yours*. Where, by the by, shall I address him?"

Chapter Fifteen

Cornwall
November 15, 1860

Dear Mr. Vaile,

I had your letter inclosed in one from my girl
Page, my stepdaughter, I should say, but I
never do because she is dear as any daughter to
me.

I thank you for the curtesey of your having
writ it, but I will abide by what Page Desides,
though hoping very much she will have you. It
would make her mother and me very happy to
see her setteled so well, and she has never

cared for anyone else but you since she was a bairn.

> *Yours respectfully,*
> *Egan Llanwelly*

> St. Ives
> November 15, 1860

My dear daughter,

It is unlike you not to be honest with yourself. You are in love with Rupert Vaile and should be overjoyed that he returns your love and wants you to be his wife. So much for your fears of his snobbery! Now, instead of accepting the man at once and telling him the truth about yourself—which is in no way shameful except to his stepmother—you are raising all manner of objections as foolish as they are false.

Page, look into your heart and acknowledge that you have been obsessed with him since you were just a child—that you went as governess to the Vailes for no other purpose but to seek him out. If it were just the money, or even because you secretly wished (which I would think only natural) to see your blood mother, you could have used the services of Mr. Wheale to arrange a meeting. You need not have gone to them in the lowly post of governess, a position hopelessly unsuitable to your pride and your high spirits.

I was aware from the start of your real object, but I thought it best to let you go without saying anything. I thought you would realize when you finally saw him that for many years you had dreamed an impossible dream. I thought you might be utterly disillusioned either by what he had become or his own indifference. I thought, above all, that it could not but be an advantage to get on with your life, having at last put him out of your heart and mind.

Instead, the dream has become a reality, he sounds everything in a man I could want for you, and he is yours for the taking.

There are no real difficulties. You can tell him the truth without enlightening his father. Just because you are marrying the future Lord Vaile does not mean that you must be like the present Lady Vaile. You can as well be a painter married as single. You can be a better sister to Eliza and Emily as their brother's wife than as their governess!

You can educate your own children at home, bring them up any way you wish, conduct your home life as you will, treat your servants however it suits you. These are the only points of difference I can see that need be discussed between you and Mr. Vaile.

Page, life is too short to throw away happiness.

> *Your loving mother,*
> *Caroline Llanwelly*

AN UNFORGOTTEN LOVE

Cliff House
November 15, 1860

Page, are you out of your mind, girl, shilly-shallying around, when you've a chance to make a fine marriage with the man you have been daft for since he was still in knickers and you were a runny-nosed brat?

Lass, if I thought it was because of us you were hesitating, I'd box your ears good and proper, I would, if I could just lay my hands on you. You have done as much and more for us than we had any reason or right to expect. I'm not saying—there being no pride between us— that when your money comes at twenty-five, we wouldn't accept more help, if needed, if it wasn't too much sacrifice for you to give it, but that's neither here nor there. We're all surviving fine as it is.

I have Cliff House for my wife and children, and there's no hurry for a new boat. I'm doing better all the time and not just at the fishing. There's a lot of transport the government blinks at, what with the war in America.

Powys would say the same about his ranch. Da and Aunt Etti are in grand shape, too, thank God, and thank you.

Maura says to tell you that it would be unkind of you to keep her bairns from being related to a lord. Unkind? It would be plain dumb.

Your loving brother,
Peter

St. Ives School
November 15, 1860

Dear Page,

For the love of heaven, use the sense the good Lord gave you and don't go on with this ploy of playing the sacrificial lamb for us.

The school is flourishing, and the expansions will come in their own good time. Aunt Etti and da keep busy and happy.

How do you think we all would feel if you threw away this chance? Exactly. So try not to be more of a fool than you can help.

Love,
Patric

The four letters had arrived together in the morning post, and Page saved her three to read during morning lessons while Eliza and Emily wrote their compositions.

A smile lingered on her lips as she folded the last short letter—Patric's—back into its envelope. Warmth filled her as she looked across at her two half sisters, the dark head and the fair one bent over their desks. How much luckier she had been than them. Her family. Her loving family.

They were pressing her hard in their letters,

168

but only for her own happiness and no harder than Rupert had been these last two weeks. He only wanted a simple *yes* before he spoke to his father, too.

Lost in a happy dream, Page hardly heard Nellie come into the room until the maid addressed her. "Miss Llanwelly, the mistress wants to see you in the morning parlor right away."

"In a pet, she is," Nellie told Page sociably as the two went downstairs together.

"What about?"

The maid's eyes rounded and her brows peaked above them. "Oh, something reel serious, a-course," she said pertly, "like maybe her new gown is an inch too long or there aren't any lobsters to be had for Friday's dinner."

Lady Vaile was reclining on a brocade lounge, velvet-shod feet up, silk-stockinged ankles crossed. She wore one of the flowered chiffon tea gowns considered appropriate for afternoon wear; there was a diamond as well as her gold wedding band on one hand, a fine emerald ring on the other. A jeweled bracelet on one wrist and several gold bangles on the other were almost hidden by the ribbons, ruching and ruffles ornamenting her sleeves as well as the neckline of her gown.

She looked up and frowned as the governess stood before her, neither speaking nor inviting her to be seated.

"You sent for me, Lady Vaile," said Page,

prepared to play and enjoy the part of Miss Llanwelly, reduced gentlewoman and governess.

"I did, indeed. I am displeased with you, Miss Llanwelly, ex-ceed-ing-ly displeased." She emphasized her displeasure as well as the words by scraping the long pointed nails of her index fingers along the brocaded arms of her lounge.

"I am sorry to hear it," Page said formally, though her eyes glittered and her nostrils flared. What an obnoxious woman this was! And, thank *you*, God, she addressed him most sincerely, for Caroline Ettington Llanwelly!

She stood, head bowed and face hidden. Let Lady Vaile mistake this attitude for one of humility and contrition instead of an attempt to hide the contempt that must be written plain on her face.

Lady Vaile did.

"I am sure you meant no harm," she said in a softened but equally patronizing manner, "but I cannot have you encouraging Miss Elizabeth in this foolish fancy she has to study painting. And to give up the harp as well! Ridiculous. There is something particularly bewitching in the sight of a lovely young woman playing the strings of a harp."

"Not," said Page tartly, her head snapping up, "if half the notes she plays are false, which I regret to say is the case with Miss Eliza. Now Em—Miss Emily, I think, might do well at the harp. *She* seems to have a good ear for music, while Eliza's talent lies elsewhere." She tried to appeal to the mother's pride and vanity. "Her painting skills are really quite remarkable."

Diane Vaile sat up very straight. She was almost more shocked than angered at the governess's poise and self-possession and her inexplicable failure to knuckle under immediately, as a proper governess should.

"Nevertheless," she ordered imperiously, "you will oblige me in this matter. I consider painting"—she wrinkled her nose as distastefully as though naming a much older profession— "a very unsuitable occupation for a lady. It is not," she added grandly and with the peculiar insensibility of the well-born to the feelings of their presumed inferiors, "as though any daughter of *mine* will ever have to seek her living as a governess or a drawing mistress."

Behind her primmed mouth, Page's teeth were grinding together to hold back an explosion of temper.

"I will excuse you this once," her sublimely unconscious mother continued, intolerably condescending, "provided that when you speak to Lord Vaile on this subject again, you tell him that, after due consideration, you think it would be in Miss Eliza's best interests to delay her drawing lessons till she is rather older."

"No," said Page bluntly, "I cannot do that. It would be a lie."

Diane's indignation actually moved her off the lounge. "Did I hear you correctly? Did you say no to *me*?"

"I did indeed."

"I will not tolerate defiance or disrespect in anyone who works for me. You will either do as I bid you or leave my employ."

"I shall tell Lord Vaile"—Page's voice rang out loud and clear; she had almost begun to enjoy herself—"that his daughter Elizabeth has an extraordinary talent, which should be nurtured and guided as soon as possible. *That* is the truth."

"Miss Llanwelly, you are dismissed. Pack your bags and go at once. You shall be paid a full month in lieu of notice."

"Oh, you needn't do that," Page said gently. "And I shan't pack my bags either. I am quite certain you will wish to rescind your dismissal after you give it some thought. You will, in fact, be eager for me to stay on and continue to educate Eliza and Emily. Who knows but that you might not be wrong about either one of them having to be a drawing mistress or a governess one day? It was, after all, what your eldest daughter had to do."

She looked without compassion into Lady Vaile's paper-white face.

"What are you saying? There is no . . . *Eliza* is my eldest daughter."

"No," Page told her cruelly. "Much as she

herself might wish otherwise, Diane Victoria Page is your eldest daughter."

Diane's face crumpled up; she looked suddenly old and far from beautiful. "You . . ." She said it again, gaspingly, "You . . ."

"That's right," said her daughter crisply, "little Vicky, last seen when I was seven. I changed my name a dozen years ago. Page for the father I never knew, Caroline for the woman who was a *real* mother to me, Llanwelly for her husband who raised me as his own."

Diane's slender blue-veined hands had been scrabbling at the ruffles about her throat, as though to pull them free to aid her breathing. "Why did you come to us?" she, whispered hoarsely.

"Why do you think—new-found mama?"

Even as Diane winced, her wits, long dulled by inaction, slowly got to working. "You want something," was her inevitable conclusion.

No tears or fatted calf for the prodigal, Page noted dispassionately.

"Money, I suppose," guessed Diane.

How are you, daughter dear, unseen for fifteen years? Not Lady Vaile. No time for such social amenities, she! Straight to the point, and the point was always the preservation of her own sweet self. Well, more than one could play at that game.

"Money. Why, of course. What else?"

"I don't have any money," Diane declared wildly.

"Now, mo-ther," Page reproached her.

"But I don't . . . truly. I can buy whatever I want, and my husband pays all the bills, but I never have any cash in hand . . . not much more than a pittance."

"Mr. Wheale said your father left you a legacy."

"There was just a few thousand pounds left when I married Lord Vaile . . . ask Mr. Wheale *that* if you don't believe me. I don't even get the interest. All these years it's been going back into the main fund for Eliza and Emily."

"But what about little Vicky in Cornwall?" Page mimicked Diane's plaintive tones. "Don't you think she should get her fair share, too?"

"But I don't—I really don't—"

Slightly sickened, both by Diane and herself, Page spoke up rather roughly. "I don't want *your* money, I want my own; but I will not get the seventy-two hundred pounds from my father's father till I am twenty-five. In case the date has slipped your mind, that's in June of 1863. I can't, however, afford to wait two and a half years. I need some money now, not the whole sum, let's say about a third. You should be able to manage a loan of twenty-five hundred pounds. It will be returned to you on my twenty-fifth birthday. With interest, if you want. Mr. Wheale can draw up a note."

"You won't listen to what I'm saying." Her agitated voice rose so shrilly that Rupert Vaile,

on his way downstairs to the study after a third
jubilant reading of the brief letter from Egan
Llanwelly, stopped on the last step to listen and
was able, without straining, to hear her final
protest. "There's no way in the world I can get
twenty-five hundred pounds for you."

He recognized the timbre of the answering
voice and strode over to the entrance of the
morning parlor just in time to hear Miss Page
Llanwelly toss off a crude suggestion. "Buy
some jewelry. You say your husband pays all
your bills. You can turn it back a few days later
for cash."

"Impossible!" gasped Diane.

"Then pawn or sell some of the jewels you
already have."

"*I*—go to a pawnbroker's!"

"Give them to me. *I'm* not too proud . . . I'll
go."

"Why are you doing this to me . . . for revenge?"

"Revenge?" Page said in a curt, clipped voice.
"No, not revenge. However unintentionally, you
did me the greatest favor in the world. I told you
what I want. Money. Or—"

Diane's hands were tearing at her throat
again. "Oh God, or you'll go to my husband,
won't you. You'll betray me—my—my—"

Page shrugged elaborately, sick and shamed,
knowing she couldn't go through with this ugly
pretense. She had started it in her old impetuous

way, spurred on by temper, and continued in hopes of getting the loan against her legacy which she no longer wanted.

"Forget it," she said wearily. "Let's both forget this conversation ever took place."

Diane misunderstood. "Oh, please," she sobbed. "Oh, please . . ."

The man in the doorway misunderstood, too.

"How much money did you want, Miss Llanwelly?"

At the sound of his voice, both women wheeled about.

Diane said, "Oh, God!" again, feeling her safe, snug world topple about her.

Page read the sentence of her guilt in the eyes staring across at her with chilling hostility; there was pronouncement of her sentence in the two words, coldly repeated, "How much?"

Her world crumbled, too.

Chapter Sixteen

He signed the check, *Rupert Vaile*, in a
hand as tight and controlled as the grim drawn
look on his face. "Twenty-five hundred pounds,"
he said aloud and rose from his desk, handing
the check to her.

"Thank you," said Page expressionlessly and
turned on her heel to leave.

"One moment, please," Rupert bade her
sharply.

"Sir?"

"I neither know nor care," Rupert told her
brusquely, "what hold you have on that vain
silly woman my father is married to, but I
assure you I am only paying you off for *his* sake. I

want your word that you will never in the future approach him in any way that will destroy his peace of mind."

"You are willing to accept *my* word?" Page baited him.

"I have to."

"Very well, then," she returned lightly. "You have it. In any event, there is now no reason to disturb Lord Vaile." She waved the check mockingly. "I have what I came for."

At the doorway she turned one more time.

"I think," she said consideringly, "you will succeed your father very nicely one day. I can see you as a very upright baron, proud and pompous, rigid and righteous . . . but not nearly so worthy of respect as he. Good-bye, my lord. Thank you for the start in life."

Her tears didn't fall, even when she was in her own room, packing. She was still too carried away on the tide of fury and indignation that had enveloped her from the moment of Rupert's quick judgment and condemnation.

"*Diavolo. Imbecille,*" she muttered below her breath. Then, shrugging, "*Meglio tardi che mai.*" Well, it *was* better to discover in time he was a stiff-necked stuffed shirt, easily turned from faith in her.

But when she thought of Eliza and Emily, her spirit faltered, her eyes filled up. What use this raging resentment that, in the beginning, had made her pursue the farce with Rupert and later kept her from breaking down as she packed?

She would be losing *them* as surely as she had already lost him. The Vailes would see to that. What would become of them? Small comfort to her young sisters that Page Llanwelly had her pride!

Under the pressure of their needs, she did what she had vowed a scant hour before she never would . . . sat down at her writing table, seized a sheet of paper and addressed a note, without salutation, to Rupert.

No matter what you think of me, you cannot doubt my honest concern for Eliza and Emily. Don't let your anger at me cause you to allow them to sink back to the situation they were in before I came to Landsdowne Hall.

Use your influence with your father to make sure the governess who succeeds me has their interests at heart, as well as a love of teaching, not just the need to achieve a snug berth and the desire to retain it by ingratiating herself with your stepmother.

Do not let Eliza's drawing talent be thrown away. Emily should be the one to study music.

Give them some of your own time and attention; you will be surprised, as you have already sometimes been, at the rewards to you.

She signed her name with a flourish, then sealed the single page in an envelope and rang for Nellie, waiting in her chair till the maid appeared.

"Nellie, I'm leaving in a short while. After I'm gone—remember, not till after that—will you see that Mr. Vaile gets this?" She handed over the envelope and two one-pound notes. "This is for you, Nellie. And thank you for everything."

"Oh, miss! Oh, my stars! You're leaving permanent?" Torn between regret at the governess's going and her joy at the two pounds, Nellie hardly knew which emotion to express.

"Yes, permanent. You *will* take good care of Miss Eliza and Miss Emily, won't you?"

"Oh, I will, Miss Llanwelly, I surely will," she promised fervently. "Here," as Page bent, "let me help you with your bag."

"Thanks, Nellie. Please leave it in the front hallway, then ask Mr. Sloan to send up a footman for my trunk and order me a hackney. I'll just step down now and say good-bye to-to the girls."

Eliza and Emily were chasing around the schoolroom throwing erasers from the blackboard at one another. They looked around guiltily when Page made her quiet entrance.

"We finished our compositions, Miss Llanwelly," Eliza told her defensively; then her eyes widened at the sight of Page's favorite plaid outdoor cape.

"Are you going somewhere, Miss Llanwelly?"

"I-I came to say good-bye to you," Page stammered, again close to tears.

"You're not coming back?" Eliza cried out on a note of panic.

Page shook her head. "I can't," she said softly.

Emily began to sob.

Page put an arm around each of her sisters and hugged them both. "Go to your brother Rupert if you need help. Talk to him if you have a problem. He'll help . . . you're not as alone as you were before."

"We th-thought you w-would m-marry Rupert," Emily wept.

"And st-stay f-forever," Eliza wailed.

"I thought so, too, for a while," Page said shakily. "It-it just didn't work out. He no longer thinks very well of me, and the truth is—right now I don't think very well of him either. But that," she added quickly, "has nothing to do with you two. He loves you both, and you can turn to him."

She gave each girl another embrace and a kiss, then fairly ran from the room, followed by their sobs and Eliza's last reproach, uttered with sorrowful dignity, "But you love him, too; I know you do."

Not bothering to deny it, Page closed the schoolroom door behind her and ran down the stairs, where a footman was waiting to carry her trunk out to the carriage.

She was standing on the pavement, while her luggage was being stowed away, when Marcus Vaile turned the corner. He approached her with his arms braced in front of him, both palms up, as though to ward off attack.

"Can I come near if I promise to behave?" he called out with cheeky good humor.

"I'm not afraid of you in public, Mr. Vaile," Page told him primly.

"You're not afraid of me anywhere," he retorted ruefully. "Ker-rist!" There was a shudder of remembrance. "Who taught you to do that?"

"My brothers. They thought any woman going out alone in the world should know how to protect herself from men willing to take advantage of her helplessness."

Faint color stained his cheeks. "Me—take advantage, yes. You—helpless, never!" he protested.

"But suppose I was, Mr. Marcus?" she asked him. "Or don't you believe the women who serve in your house should have the right to say no? Or that the defenseless deserve protection from being preyed on against their will?"

"Lesson learned, Miss Llanwelly. I assure you, it was learned most painfully. I am glad of this encounter because I have been wanting"—his gray eyes gazed earnestly into hers, for once neither mocking nor flirtatious—"to make my apologies to you. I am most sincerely and abjectly sorry." He reached out and lightly tapped one shoulder. "Forgiven?" he beseeched winningly.

He sounded younger and more beguiling than his sisters begging for a treat. Page could not help smiling. "Forgiven," she agreed.

"Your baggage is stacked, miss," said the footman, gladly accepting a coin along with her thanks.

"You're leaving us?" Marcus asked. "But I thought you and Rupert—"

"No," said Page firmly. She held out her hand, and he shook it heartily. "Rupert and I are *not*. Good-bye, Mr. Marcus."

He helped her into the carriage. "Shall I tell the driver your destination?"

Page smiled faintly. "Thank you. I'll tell him presently."

After one last wave of her hand, she sat back against the cushions, so wrapped up in her far-from-happy thoughts that the coachman had to swivel his head around and ask twice for information before she came out of her reverie long enough to answer him. "The Devane Art Gallery in Pimlico."

She had the hackney wait while she went inside to inquire for the home address of Paolo Lorenzo.

The manager of the gallery, a tall, skinny man in an elegant evening frock coat, told her self-importantly, "We cannot give information about Mr. Lorenzo to any stranger who demands it."

"I am Miss Page Llanwelly," she answered haughtily, "no stranger to Mr. Lorenzo. I am a student and relation of Antonio Grazzi, Mr. Lorenzo's colleague and dear friend. Only a few weeks ago, by Mr. Lorenzo's personal invitation, I attended his opening exhibit here. He asked me then to contact him at his home," she lied, "but most unfortunately, I lost the paper on which the direction was written down. I have a letter from Mr. Grazzi to deliver to him."

This much was true, and by way of proof, she produced a square white envelope on which was scribbled in a foreign-looking script, *Signore P. Lorenzo.*

Quelled by her commanding manner, the manager supplied Lorenzo's address and Page hurried back to the waiting carriage.

Arrived at a tall narrow stone house not more than a half mile from the gallery, Page once again told the coachman to wait. A black-clad housekeeper, who spoke heavily accented English, eyed her letter suspiciously and at last reluctantly agreed to take it to the master in his studio.

Page snatched the envelope back. "No," she told the housekeeper in faultless Italian. "I must take it to him myself. Those were my instructions."

The housekeeper beamed all over her face. *"Sia lodato Iddio!* An English miss who speaks so perfectly the Italian of Rome. Come, my little bird, the master will eat us both, but you yourself shall bring the letter to him."

The entire top floor of the house was given over to Lorenzo's studio. Page's eyes sparkled at the sight of it. The smell of paint and oils was more exciting to her than the finest French perfume; the sight of easels and paintbrushes and carelessly stacked canvases was so dear and familiar, happy tears stood in her eyes. She had missed it sorely these last months, when time and space had permitted only the tamest sketching and drawing.

A third of the roof of the house seemed to have been torn away to permit the insertion of long panes of glass, which gave entrance to as much London daylight as a gray November day could provide. On a raised dais at the end of the room, a blowsily pretty, redhaired woman with a plump rounded stomach stood bent over a tub of water, her generous breasts overflowing from the top of a short chemise, her pink bottom protruding from it below.

Paolo Lorenzo—Page recognized him at once from Antonio's vivid description—was slapping color onto his canvas with slashing paint strokes, at the same time lustily singing a ribald Italian love song. He was a wisp of a man with bright blue eyes, a great beak of a nose and a mop of tight blond curls. His filthy green cotton painter's smock had the sleeves pulled out; his courduroy trousers were cut off at the thighs, revealing skinny legs, knobby knees and bare dirty feet.

When Page and the housekeeper entered, he stopped singing but continued painting, while exclaiming dramatically, "Caterina, why do you interrupt me? How many times must I tell you, I am not to be interrupted?"

"The interruption is my fault, Signore Lorenzo," Page told him in English, amused and not troubling to conceal it. Then she switched to Italian. "Antonio Grazzi bid me come and see you, master. I have a letter for you from him."

He had ignored her first remark in English. On hearing "the Italian of Rome," he cast down his brush and condescended to turn around, inspecting her from head to foot.

The model on the dais straightened up, with a gusty sigh of relief, stretched her arms wide, wriggled her shoulders, then sank down on a hassock, scratching at her left breast.

Lorenzo advanced on Page and peered up into her face, uttering a very English, "Hah!" He continued to study her, following up with, "Hmm."

"Give me the letter!" he demanded finally, and Page handed over the square white envelope.

186

Chapter Seventeen

THE CAREFULLY TREASURED LETTER FROM ROME
had been read and tossed aside with something
of disdain.

"Antonio tells me you are his most promising
pupil." He thumped his bony chest. "Me, Lorenzo, the greatest painter of them all today, I do
not believe it. *Women*"—he snorted out the word
like a curse—"they do not have the heart"—he
rapped his own—"or the brains"—he tapped his
head—"or the genius"—he threw up his hands.
"They are only fit for making squiggles on a
piece of paper. Why do you not stick to painting
daffodils on plates and violets on vases?" He

made another elaborate gesture of disdain. "Pah. Coloring on china. That is what women are fit for."

"*Ascolami bene. Chese cosa avete,*" Page shouted back, then added several fluent Italian curses, at which Lorenzo's eyes opened wide and the housekeeper's eyes closed while she crossed herself. "Like most men," she accused him fiercely, "you speak much and say nothing. You believe what you want to believe. You would like to dismiss the gifts of women so arbitrarily in order to get rid of their competition. Well, for your information, I have the heart and the brains to be as great a painter as any. Give me a few years," she finished as arrogantly as he, "and I will gladly match *my* genius against *yours!*"

Lorenzo, far from being angered by this attack, laughed in delight. "You have passion!" he exclaimed. "That is good. You are not the prim English miss you seem. Take off your bonnet."

"Ahhh." He gave a prolonged sigh of pleasure when Page immediately obliged him. Then he came close and peered up into her eyes and poked one forefinger against her cheek. "Take off your cloak." Page tossed it over the back of a chair.

"Ahhh."

He glanced over at the redhaired model, still sitting on the edge of the dais, smiling vacuously and now scratching vigorously at her navel.

He turned back to Page.

"Did you know that Antonio asked in his letter for Lorenzo to teach you?" he asked her.

She nodded.

"You ask, too? You want that Paolo Lorenzo should teach you?"

"Very much."

"*Molte bene.* Then I shall. For one month, every day, you will paint, and I shall criticize and instruct. If I—the great Lorenzo—decide that you have the gift, *bene,* then you stay. If you do not have the-the—*como se diche?*—the touch, then you may go back to Grazzi. Me, I do not waste my time on nothings. Caterina, prepare a room for—*come si chiana?*"

"*Mi chiama* Page. Page Llanwelly."

"Pa-age. Bah! I cannot say such a name. I will call you Pasqua."

He put his hands on his hips and surveyed her with a deep scowl. "You hesitate. You blush. You are afraid to stay with Lorenzo. No, no, little miss, you have nothing to fear." Deep laughter rumbled up from his belly and out of his throat. "Paolo Lorenzo no makes the love with little English virgins who know nothing. For my bed, I want such as she." He stabbed a forefinger toward the dais. "Lots of woman and good strong muscles and stupid like the cow."

Page's blush deepened, the redhaired model's empty smile widened to a grin, and Lorenzo smiled beamingly at them all. "Caterina shall be your chaperone. She shall sit with you even when you pose for me. You may go now . . . *ilo molto lavoro arretrato.*"

He turned back to his easel.

"When I . . . what did you say?"

Once more he flung down his brush. "You object?" he shouted. "I shall give you your place to stay and meals and Caterina, too, to preserve your chastity. You cannot call yourself a painter and be ashamed to show to Lorenzo, who shall make it immortal, the beautiful body the good God gave you!"

"I never said I was ashamed!" Page retorted with spirit.

"*Bene.* Then you pose now. Take off your clothes. You!" He addressed the model. "Go. *Abaso.* Eat something in the kitchen. I see you later."

He advanced on Page, who was slowly unbuttoning the top of her gown, and with his two hands yanked it all the way down to her waist. "Ahhh, the bosom fills out the chemise, *bellissima.* Keep on the chemise, perhaps one petticoat, if it is transparent. Nothing else. We want the hips and the limbs to show. You are a lady making ready for the bath. You should looked touched—touchable? Above all, desired . . . that is the English word, yes?"

"Desirable?" Page offered diffidently, stepping out of her gown.

"Ahhh, *desirable,* sì. When I paint you, Pasqua, you shall not look like the English virgin but like the desirable woman, flesh and blood and"—he kissed his fingers to her and rolled his eyes—"and delicious rounded curves. Now, take off the shoes and stockings and then the petticoats. No, all of them. They are too thick. I will make ready the canvas."

He ignored her, fussing over his easel until he was ready. Then he beckoned her over to the dais to have the pose set. First, he placed her standing near the tub, arm stretched up, then standing, bending over. Next he had her kneeling. No pose seemed to please him.

"How do you see it?" Page asked him finally.

He muttered Sicilian curses. "I want the length of one leg—*Dio!* your legs!—and at the same time, the curve here and there"—with his paint brush he lightly slapped her hip and buttock. "Also a glimpse of bosom."

He pondered, then instructed in rapid Italian. "Picture it thus. Your lover is looking at your back view, and you all innocent and unknowing —the English miss—but your body tells a different story. The body is his for the taking even if the English miss is unaware."

Page closed her eyes, blanking out the room so as to see more vividly the picture he had drawn.

When she opened her eyes, she was smiling. She went to the tub and stood against it on her left leg, kneeling with her right on the edge of the tub, bending over, far over, giving him the curve of hip and buttock he had asked for and a tantalizing glimpse of one breast, halfway out of the chemise, the other covered by a hanging strand of hair, her arms plunged down in the water up to her elbows.

"The lady has prepared her bath," came her muffled voice, "but she dropped the soap and is trying to find it before she removes the chemise. All the curves you want are showing."

"*Meraviglioso!* Perhaps it is true, after all, you have the brains to paint," he acknowledged with another lusty laugh. "Tomorrow we see, but today you pose. Do not move a muscle. Caterina, get out of my way. Go where I cannot see you. Pasqua," he warned from his easel, "if you lose the pose, I shall push your head under the water and drown you like a kitten. But, *sta quieto* and, after breakfast in the morning, you shall show me your work and then we paint together. Sì?"

"Sì," agreed Page, but an hour later, she gasped out, "Signore, I must rest. My hands are turning into prunes, and in another minute I shall slip into the water myself."

"Wait one minute more." He added a final few strokes. "Now, let me study the pose. Ah, *bene.* Now, Pasqua, you may have the rest."

Page flopped into the nearest chair, groaning, just as Caterina, who had slipped out twenty minutes before, came back to announce lunch.

She reached for her petticoats, but Caterina stopped her, walking over to a wardrobe and returning with a long red satin Chinese robe embroidered back and front with dragons. "This will be more comfortable, my little bird."

Page slipped into the robe thankfully and followed the master downstairs. Lorenzo allowed her fifteen minutes to walk around, working off a huge Italian lunch of fish, veal in wine sauce and pasta, before he had her posing again.

He kept her at it mercilessly till the light was gone, then threw down his brush. "*Ecco fatto. Avanti*," he invited. "Look, I have made much progress. Well, what do you think?" he asked as Page just stared and stared.

"Signore Lorenzo, I know it's me," she gasped, "but I . . . but I . . ."

"How do you see yourself, English miss?"

It was easier to say in Italian. "Innocent . . . and wanton, both," Page told him, with one hand against her burning cheek, the other trying to pull her chemise up higher.

The next day she brought all the sketch pads and drawings she had with her up to the studio and sat quietly while Lorenzo slowly studied them, one by one. Sometimes he said, "Pah!" or screwed up his nose as though at a bad smell, sending Page's heart spiraling down, down, down. Several times he hummed a little or muttered, "Ahhh," and then for a moment, till his next frown, the pressure inside her eased.

He came and stood before her when he was done. "Not so much talent as you boast," he told her almost reprovingly, "certainly none to compare with Lorenzo's . . . but you are good, yes, you are good," he acknowledged ungrudgingly, "and the heart and the brains, you have them, too, as well as the passion."

He clapped her heartily and impersonally on the behind.

"It is agreed then—I teach you and you pose for me and Caterina feeds you and keeps you English virgin?"

"It is agreed," Page sniffled happily.

"Take off your clothes," said Lorenzo in great good humor. "First we pose." He went over to the door of the studio. "Caterina! Caterina!" he roared. "Bring up your fat bottom from the kitchen. The English miss poses for me."

The next two months Page worked harder than she ever had in her life. They rose early to catch the morning light, and after a hearty breakfast, hurried up to the studio where for two to three hours, with only brief rests, she posed for him.

After *Lady Looking For Her Soap*, he painted *Lady In Her Bath*. For this one she sat in a slouching pose in the tub, immersed to just above her nipples, her face looking freshly and rosily scrubbed, her hair twisted into a knot on the top of her head, and one of the long legs Lorenzo was enchanted with raised straight in the air while she bent forward to wash it, a bar of soap in one hand, a sponge in the other.

After lunch they painted together, using the same model, for a few weeks the one with red hair, then an even plumper blonde, and after her a change-of-pace petite sloe-eyed beauty with black hair down to her knees and a most disconcerting cockney accent.

It was no secret that Paolo Lorenzo took all his models to bed, since he did so with the loud, lusty gusto he brought to his painting. Page soon learned to spare herself embarrassment by retiring to the kitchen with Caterina whenever the master was not alone in his bedroom.

Their evenings were very social. Lorenzo was known to keep Open House, and other painters, students and all sorts and conditions of people connected in any way with the world of art dropped in without the ceremony of invitation. Page suspected the impecunious among them came as much for Caterina's coffee and pastries and pasta as to sit at the feet of the master.

There were parties to attend, too; occasional exhibits at the Royal Academy, many more at the private galleries.

All in all, life at Lorenzo's gave Page little time to brood over the love she had lost almost as soon as it had been found. When she thought of Rupert, it was always with a pang of grief; when she remembered Eliza and Emily, it was with an ache about her heart. . . .

But then a moment afterward, Paolo Lorenzo would be shouting, *"Venga subita;* we must take advantage of the light," or "Why do you change expression? Smile. Dream. You are happy, thinking of your lover who comes soon."

Even at night, when she might have lain

awake, reliving the agony of that one moment when Rupert had judged and condemned her, she was so exhausted from the long, hard-working day that, almost before she could settle down for a good cry, her eyes would close. She would sleep the sorrow away.

Chapter Eighteen

DURING THE FIRST WEEKS AFTER MISS PAGE Llanwelly's departure from their house, Rupert was forced to suffer the disapproval of all his siblings as well as the pangs of disappointed love. He was out of favor not only with his young half sisters but, surprisingly, with his brother, too.

Eliza and Emily made their feelings clear by an unsmiling stiffness of manner in his presence. Marcus was far more vocal and direct.

Coming straight from the street and his parting with Page to the study where Rupert still sat at his desk, head in hands, he soon had the whole story out of him.

"Rupert, you're a fool. That girl is no extortionist."

"Good God! Do you think I *want* to believe it? But I heard her with my own ears."

"I would sooner believe your ears had played you false than that the spirited young woman who once"—he closed his eyes, shuddering—"who once kneed me in the groin and just one quarter of an hour ago delivered a brief lecture to me on the manners and morals expected of the gentry, would try to obtain money in any such tortuous fashion." He snorted contemptuously. "Lord, Rupert, I think your wits have gone begging. That is one hellishly bright girl. And you are saying that, for twenty-five hundred pounds—only a very small part of the money our grandmother left you, not to mention the much larger amount and the properties and title that will be yours one day—she jeopardized her chance to bag the lot. Not bloody likely."

Shaken, but stubborn, Rupert persisted. "She may have had some immediate need for cash ... and remember, I was not supposed to find out. If Diane hadn't lost her head and started throwing loud hysterics, I might still remain in blissful ignorance."

Marcus looked at him rather pityingly.

"I would say you still remain in blissful ignorance, old fellow. That girl could no more—why, she is the most painfully direct woman I have ever encountered." He grinned. "In point of fact, meeting her *was* damned painful," he reminded Rupert. The grin faded and he shook his head. "You used to be quite a gay dog in your Oxford days. What happened to you in the East? Did you spend so much time among dead bones, your natural instincts withered?"

"There are plenty of charming women in the East," Rupert retorted, not without asperity. "Abundantly available, lovely . . . docile . . . my great mistake was thinking I had come home to find one so bewitchingly different from all the others."

"I think you did, brother." Seeing Rupert's face, he changed his tack. "Have you questioned Diane?"

"I tried. Our charming idiot of a stepmother would only weep and beg me not to distress father with a long-past peccadillo that could only bring him trouble and sorrow. I don't intend to," he added curtly.

Identical cynical smiles appeared on both their faces; it was one of the rare times when the family resemblance between them was marked.

"Do you suppose," Marcus asked thoughtfully, "our revered stepmama has actually ever exerted herself to the point of taking a lover?"

"Just so long as she doesn't do anything to disturb father in the future. I made it quite clear"—Rupert's voice took on the inflexible note which no doubt, Marcus thought regretfully, he had used to alienate Miss Llanwelly—

"that my continued silence depended on her future good behavior."

After a few weeks when Lord Vaile, with his son's help, had found a pleasant day school which his daughters could attend mornings, and also, at Rupert's behest, the harp and music master had been transferred to Emily and a drawing master found for Eliza, both girls began to thaw a little. They even consented to attend a theatre matinee with him and afterward graciously accepted his invitation to tea at the Clarendon. Over a bountiful meal, they chattered to him with ease about their new school and their new friends, and he ventured to ask about the new drawing master.

"He will do for now," Eliza said, pokering up again. "He does *not* draw as well as Miss Llanwelly, of course."

She selected another sandwich from the plate and passed it across to Emily. They ignored Rupert for several moments, their manner delivering a silent but obvious message. He might in time be forgiven, but his offense was far from forgotten.

Several days later, as the family sat at breakfast, Lord Vaile distributed the morning mail and Rupert opened a statement from his bank. He frowned a little over the final column of figures and then ruffled through a sheaf of checks. Marcus, watching him, noticed the sudden pallor of his face; but Rupert, recollecting himself, put the statement aside and turned to his letters.

When the meal was over, he signaled Marcus with his eyes, and his brother followed him out of the room and upstairs.

A maid was making up his bed. He sent her away with a brusqueness most unlike him. Later, in the servants' hall, she reported the episode with exaggerated drama. "Dead-white he was—coo! He was the color of the sheets. And that dis-trawt, you wouldn't believe. Something's happened, it has."

In his bedroom, meanwhile, Rupert's pale face and distracted manner might have lent some substance to the housemaid's claims.

"Mark, she never cashed the check I gave her."

"After nearly four weeks?" Marcus's eyebrows lifted. "Strangely dilatory for an extortionist, wouldn't you say?"

"Oh God, Mark! I don't even know where she is."

"She took care that last day not to let me find out where she was going," Marcus said thoughtfully. "How about her letters of reference—or any mail from her home? She came from Cornwall . . . is that all you know?"

Rupert stopped pacing, went to a small desk and opened the top drawer. "This letter is from her father. She told me once he was a Truro man, but the letter is postmarked St. Ives."

"I don't know how hard or easy it would be tracing a Llanwelly in St. Ives or Truro, but they would be a starting point, wouldn't they?"

"Yes, of course, I could go—good God!" Rupert suddenly smote his left palm with a clenched right fist. "She was referred to us originally by a solicitor. Mr.—ah—Wiley? No, no, it was Wheale, that's it, Mr. Wheale. He handled Diane's affairs . . . the money she had from her father and her first marriage."

"Diane would know where you can locate him then," Marcus offered practically.

"Diane. Of course."

He punched Marcus joyfully on the shoulders and tore downstairs, taking the steps two at a time, adding further fuel to the blaze of gossip going on in the kitchen.

It was necessary to dry Diane's tears and persuade her that his proposed visit to Mr. Wheale had nothing to do with her and would in no way involve her in unpleasantness.

"I am only trying to trace Miss Llanwelly's whereabouts," he blundered as reassurance when the desired information was finally produced. Diane began to weep all over again. In a fever of impatience to be gone, this time he summoned her maid to offer aid and comfort and clean handkerchiefs.

After a forty-minute wait in the solicitor's office, Rupert was ushered in by a clerk and greeted by Mr. Wheale with an outward air of calm courtesy. Inwardly, the solicitor was seething with curiosity.

"Mr. Vaile." They shook hands. "I was sorry to have to keep you waiting so long."

"My fault entirely, sir." Rupert smiled charmingly. "I was too impatient to make an appointment in the ordinary way. I am anxious—I am trying—Mr. Wheale, can you tell me where I may find Page Llanwelly?"

"I know where she presently resides, sir, but—"

"That's all I want to know," Rupert interrupted, a smile of mixed joy and relief spreading over his face.

"But I can't tell you," concluded the solicitor. "I have been requested by my client not to give that information to anyone—particularly anyone named Vaile."

All the blood left Rupert's face and then surged back again in a hot shamed tide of color.

"Particularly *me,* I assume?"

Mr. Wheale inclined his head in acknowledgment.

"She told you what happened between us?"

"She did." There was accusation in the voice if not the words.

"What else could I think?" Rupert defended himself. "I heard her *demanding* money of my stepmother, suggesting she sell her jewelry to get it. She sounded . . . greedy . . . vulgar . . . utterly unlike the woman I had come to—she—

what else was I to think?" he repeated without
conviction.

"That is a matter for you and your conscience,
Mr. Vaile," Mr. Wheale told him, not unkindly.
"If she behaved as you say. . . . But knowing
Miss Llanwelly as I do . . . her kindness, her
loyalty, her sense of honor. In all truth, it is hard
for me to believe in the woman you have just
described," he finished more austerely. "Nevertheless, my hands are tied. I have my instructions, and I—"

"I understand, Mr. Wheale. I cannot fault you.
I shall just have to go on with my first plan,
which was to journey to St. Ives and Truro.
Thank you for your time. Good day to you, sir."

His hand was on the doorknob when Mr.
Wheale spoke again.

"Mr. Vaile. I think it would be a mistake for
you to go to St. Ives, sir. It is too soon."

"Too *soon*?"

"Her family may have been told—the same as
I—not to inform you where *in London* she is
living. No matter if one of them goes against her
instructions. She was hurt by your lack of faith
in her, sir. I might even say she was devastated.
The anger that came afterward—well, in many
ways, it was a protection against that hurt.
Which is not to say she lacks a temper. She has a
rather fierce one. And she does not forgive easily
those who injure her or hers."

"What are you trying to say, Mr. Wheale?"

"If you go to her before her anger has cooled

ufficiently—and it has not—you may irrepara-
ly damage a relationship that may yet be saved.
f you will be patient . . . just a little longer . . . I
will help you."

"*How* long?" Rupert asked reasonably, thank-
ul for the hint that Page was in London.

Mr. Wheale hesitated. "A month?"

"God, no!" Rupert exclaimed in a voice of
uppressed violence. "I could not wait so
ong."

"Three weeks . . . *two?*"

"One!" Rupert countered firmly. "One only—
r I go to St. Ives."

"Very well, Mr. Vaile," Mr. Wheale capitu-
ated. "Within one week, one way or another,
ou may expect to hear from me."

> *Farringdon Street*
> *27 December, 1860*

My dear Mr. Vaile,

*I must abide by the wishes of my client that I
ot divulge her present place of residence. This
ecision ensures the scrupulous upholding of
he letter of the law.*

*In line with your request, however, the en-
losed invitation may, perhaps, be of assis-
ance to you, without any violation on my part
f client confidentiality.*

> *Very truly yours,*
> *George L. Wheale*

AN UNFORGOTTEN LOVE

Rupert seized eagerly at the card of invitation

Esibizione Di Quadri

by

Paolo Lorenzo of Rome
and his English Pupils

Private Presentation for three days
prior to Public Display

January 3,4,5, 1861
Devane Gallery
Pimlico

"Good lord!" said Rupert softly. "Of course. I
should have figured it out myself." He re-read
the invitation. "January third. Less than a
week." He folded the card in his breast pocket, a
sudden silly happy smile upon his face.

Chapter Nineteen

THE DEVANE GALLERY WAS BUZZING WITH sound and packed with people when Rupert Vaile entered with his two young sisters in tow. There were a dozen small clusters of people gathered about the paintings, talking loudly together and gesticulating with energy. There was a student group, catalogues in hand, listening earnestly to their lecturer; some casual droppers-in; a few art critics and an even fewer serious buyers . . . but not Page Llanwelly.

"It's early yet," Eliza said with one of the flashes of intuition that could still surprise her brother. "Let's look at the pictures while we wait. Let's start this—oh, my gracious!"

"What's the matter?" Rupert looked in the same direction as she toward two large canvases that seemed to be the focal point of the exhibition. The student group, pressing forward just at that moment, blocked out the view that had caused Eliza's face to screw up so strangely, as though she were not quite sure whether to laugh or to cry.

"What's the matter, Elizabeth?" Rupert asked again quietly, starting toward the painting.

A hand on his arm held him back. A voice of quiet desperation asked, "Rupert, you *know* how you feel about your fossils?"

"Well, of course . . ."

"That's how Miss Llanwelly feels about painting and—and the human f-form. She doesn't think we should be ashamed of our bodies any more than you are of your—of the naked bones you dig up in the cavern. That's why she thought it was perfectly ordinary to take us swimming with hardly anything on"—her voice pitched higher and higher—"and why, on those hot nights last summer, she said, 'Don't be silly, why smother yourself in nightgowns.'" She turned to her sister. "Tell him, Emily."

Bewildered, but compliant, Emily obliged with, "Oh yes, Rupert, Miss Llanwelly thinks bodies are beautiful." Warming up to this theme, she added, "She always said it wasn't fair that Adam was the one to eat the apple while women got punished with whalebone corsets."

At another time Rupert might have been amused. Not now. With a sense of foreboding inspired by Eliza's badgered look, he pushed his way through the students, followed by indignant murmurs from those he had jostled out of the way.

He planted himself in the front row in time to hear the lecturer declaiming ". . . the strong sensual appeal of all his subjects but a great deal more subtle and finer-drawn. Notice this curve of hip and thigh as she bends, the taut muscles of the buttock . . . typical Lorenzo."

"*Not* the breast only half out of the chemise, though!" one of the students spoke up.

"Or the other hidden by her hair!" piped up a voice just behind Rupert. "He usually shows everything there is to show, not just tantalizing glimpses."

"Too true," laughed the lecturer, "but if you will observe . . ."

Rupert never learned what next he was supposed to observe. He had already observed too much, and the effect had been to send him into a murderous rage.

He had seen once and forever since cherished in the private recesses of his memory that selfsame line of hip and thigh, the taut muscles of her buttock, as she bent over. He had dreamed of the moment when those ripe breasts would be unveiled for his own delight. *Solely* for his own delight. Not to be stared at with a greedy enjoy-

ment meant to pass for aesthetic appreciation,
then publicly dissected, gossiped and laughed about by voracious-eyed rapacious-tongued
strangers!

He felt a tug on both his arms and looked down
to glare, glad of a target on which to vent his
fury, but the tuggers were Eliza and Emily.

"They are very good paintings of her," Eliza
said with unwonted meekness.

"My goodness!" Emily studied the first painting with greater care. "*Lady Looking For Her
Soap*," she read aloud. "Is it really Miss Llanwelly?" she whispered to her sister.

"I suppose so."

Doubtfully. . . . "It does look like her hair."

"Her hair!" hissed Eliza in righteous exasper-
ation. "Emily, don't be a donkey. Look at the
lines of her body. You can't mistake them. It's
her!"

"I don't see how the *lines* can tell you."

But Rupert wasn't listening. He was staring
instead at the original of the painting. She was
standing in the doorway, the beautiful, *un*mis-
takable lines of her body decorously covered by a
ruby-red velvet gown with a modest crinoline,
long sleeves and a wide lacy Puritan-style collar
with little ties all the way to her throat.

Her escort was the most extraordinary little
man wearing wide-bottomed black velvet trousers and a flowing pink silk shirt with a huge
bow at his neck. His head of tight blond curls,
like an old Roman sculpture, was not much

higher than Page's shoulder; his face was all big nose and burning blue eyes.

Rupert once again pushed his way through the students, his sisters following. Free of the group, the three stationed themselves in a corner and he fastened his unblinking stare so fixedly on Page, she finally was impelled to turn toward them.

Recognizing Rupert at the same moment that his sisters recognized her, Page's face turned the shade of the ruby-red gown. Her former pupils rushed forward and flung themselves at her, shrieking loudly and joyously, "Miss Llanwelly!"

Bent low, an arm around each girl, Page looked up at their brother, arriving only seconds behind them.

"Good afternoon, Mr. Vaile," she said sedately.

"Good afternoon, Miss Llanwelly," he said with such extraordinary expressionless courtesy, she knew at once that he must have seen Lorenzo's semi-nudes of her.

Feeling a perverse and vaguely frightened enjoyment of his displeasure, Page asked airily, "Have you looked at the exhibit?"

Emily spoke up with a tactlessness that made Eliza gasp. "We saw the paintings of you. You know, the one where you're looking for your soap in the water and the other of you in the tub."

Page turned to Eliza. "Did you like them?" she asked, as one painter to another.

"Oh, yes." Eliza sighed ecstatically. "Mr. Lorenzo is a wonderful painter, isn't he? If I could only work with someone like him one day."

"Perhaps you can," Page encouraged her. "I'm studying with him now."

"Do you have any paintings in this exhibit, Miss Llanwelly?"

"Not paintings." Page hesitated. "I'm working on a nude right now for the next exhibit. It's of a young runner . . . a beautiful boy." She was still speaking to Eliza, but Rupert knew the words were for his benefit. "I call it *Modern Olympian*. This exhibit was planned before I went to live with Lorenzo, so all I had time for was a series of sketches—almost cartoons. They're down at that end." She pointed. "On the left."

"Come on, Emily, let's go see."

Emily hesitated, preferring to stay with her beloved Miss Llanwelly. "*Emily*." Eliza pinched her arm. "Come *on*."

"*Living* with Lorenzo?" Rupert said in a voice of soft fury the moment they were alone.

Page tipped up her chin.

"In *his* house as *his* student with a dragon named Caterina—*his* housekeeper—as chaperone, if," she added flippantly, "it matters to you."

"It matters very much." The anger had all gone; there was naked love and longing in Rupert's voice as he stepped nearer to her. "Page," he said—then, in a voice graveled and unsteady,

"Dear Page, I have missed you so. Why didn't you cash my check?"

"I never intended to."

"Then why did you take it?" he asked roughly. "Why did you make me think the worst of you?"

Page's mouth twisted up in remembered pain and bitterness. "As I recall, *you* thought the worst without any help from me. I suppose, at the time"—she shrugged—"it seems so long ago now . . . I just wanted to fulfill your worst expectations. You seemed to accept them so readily, who was I to disillusion you?"

"I am not excusing myself," Rupert told her doggedly. "I know that I—but Page, try to look at it from my viewpoint. I heard you demanding money from her—twenty-five hundred pounds was the sum Diane mentioned—I *heard* you tell her to have my father buy her some jewelry which could be returned to the store for cash. I heard you offer to go to a pawnbroker's and . . ."

"You heard the governess trying to extort money from one of her betters, and that was all you needed," Page told him very quietly. "I acknowledge the circumstances and the conversation were both very damning, but you were supposed to be madly in love with me. You—"

"I *am* madly in love with you."

"You could have *asked* me what it was all about," Page swept on, though her heightened color showed a certain consciousness about his interruption. "Shaken it out of me even. You could have demanded, 'What the hell are you up to, Miss Llanwelly?'"

She looked away from him, her hands beating a nervous tattoo against her sides. "I admit I was playing a rather unpleasant game. I don't like your stepmother, and she—I—I'm not very proud either of—of—but I would never condemn anyone I was supposed to love the way that you did me. No questions, no trial—just a swift one-man conviction."

"Forgive me." Rupert's hand went out to her. "Please forgive me, Page."

After what seemed like a long while, Page accepted the hand, and his fingers closed so convulsively around hers, she gasped in pain.

"Sorry." But he pressed her fingers again before releasing them.

"I do . . . I have forgiven it, but—"

"I still want to marry you, Page. I have never stopped."

"I can't," Page told him wretchedly.

"Can't?"

"It was a mistake thinking I ever could."

"May I know why?" he asked with awful politeness.

"My painting is as important to me as your fossils are to you. I could never give it up, any more than you could give up your scientific digging."

"I would never ask you to."

"I have years more study . . . I couldn't stay

all the time in Derbyshire, where your cavern is."

"I don't stay there all year myself, you may have noticed. We could divide our time between Derbyshire and London. While I am digging, you could paint. And when you studied in London, so could I. There is much research and museum work that I could do in town."

"I could never live under your father's roof. Much as I respect him, I could never accept the restrictions and rules he places on the women of his household."

"I never expected you could. I have a substantial income of my own. We could well afford a London house."

"You don't—you won't understand. I want—to be free."

"Free?"

"I have lived on my own for so many years, pleasing only myself. For . . . for . . . well, for instance, how would you feel, if we were married, about my posing for Lorenzo?"

"Now that," he admitted very gently, "I confess I would not consent to."

"Consent!" Page pounced on that innocuous word, almost as though she was waiting for a signal to justify her outburst. "That's just what I mean. You consider that marriage would give you the right to withhold your consent to something *I* chose to do. I don't agree. You might be justified in objecting—even though I should, of course, pay your objections no heed. But *consent!* Why should you have the right of consent over *my* actions? Would you give up digging for fossils if I withheld my permission to keep on with it?"

"The two cases are hardly the same!"

"Are they not? You know as well as I do, if you are honest, that your society regards all that digging and the bones as much a folly as my painting and posing."

"I *do* know, and I don't care a snap of my fingers. There is, however, a difference between folly and the blatant exhibition of one's body."

"In *my* eyes, Rupert, there is no such blatant exhibition. Doesn't that prove to you how very unsuited we are?"

"No," he told her rather grimly. "It just proves to me that you uttered some meaningless words before. You have not really forgiven me, and one means you are employing to punish me, even if you choose to cover it up with artistic mumbo-jumbo, is by flaunting to the world that which I would want—*hope* was for my eyes only . . . yourself."

The color of her gown was again indistinguishable from the skin tone of her face; his combined accusation and reproach, no less than his sardonic eye, had for once in her life left her totally tongue-tied. Mercifully for Page, Eliza and Emily came scampering back at this point.

Eliza appeared rather thoughtful, but Emily

was laughing. "There was a lady in one of the pictures who looked like mama," she reported to Rupert. "And there was a man who sort of looked like Marcus, only fat. He was funny."

"They weren't meant to be anyone in particular, Emily," Page said so hastily that it was Rupert's turn to look thoughtful.

"I mustn't go without seeing your paintings," he told her blandly.

"They're nothing—just pencil sketches. I'll be glad to have you see what I'm doing for the next exhibit. There are some wonderful landscapes over here—Peter Chisholm's. Perhaps you've heard of him," she rattled on, trying to steer them all to the right side of the room. "He's been written up in the *Art Journal* as one of the most promising of the new young English painters. He comes to Lorenzo's studio every day."

"I would like to look at Chisholm's work." Page drew a deep relieved breath. "*After* I see your sketches," he continued smoothly. She gulped and grimaced at Eliza, who telegraphed back mute sympathy.

Page looked wildly about as her sisters trailed after their brother. Across the room Peter Chisholm, a hulking young man, and another male student were talking to Paolo Lorenzo. With a strong instinct for self-preservation, she dashed over and eased herself firmly into the center of the group.

Ten minutes later Rupert Vaile came march-

ing up to them, his face a careful blank. Th
presence of her group did not seem to concern (
to inhibit him.

"I believe I have just seen another part of th
punishment," he told her, eyebrows quirked, bu
not unpleasantly. Page's breathing eased.

"As I recall," he went on softly, "a short whil
ago you rebuked me for my failure to inquire int
your conduct and motives on another occasio
when I rather thought that both were dubious.

His friendly smile embraced Lorenzo and th
other two students as well as Page. "I shall no
fall into the same error twice," he assured he
almost caressingly. "Now what were your in
structions? Ah yes, that I shake it out of you,
believe."

Upon which, he proceeded to take her by he
velvet-clad shoulders and shake her with grea
energy.

With her head shaking back and forth like
rag mop having the dust beat out of it, Page ha
little time to observe that he was looking fa
more amused than angry until he was don
with the shaking and had stepped away fron
her.

"Now . . . let me see . . . what was suppose
to come next?" He pretended to consider, eve
as a breathless Page fluttered her hands towar
a growling Peter to indicate that she was wel
able to take care of this situation herself.

"I believe I was supposed to ask," Ruper

mused, "what the hell this is all about. So I *do* ask it, Miss Llanwelly. I ask it just as bluntly as you suggested." She gave a nervous start at the sudden sharp change in his voice. "Page, you little vixen, just what the devil are you up to?"

Chapter Twenty

Art Journal, February 1861

Extract from the column, *London Views,* by Maurice Froman Jowett:

... work of the students, without a doubt, dominated by Peter Chisholm's landscapes, but a new and promising talent was unveiled with the showing of a series of sketches by another of Mr. Lorenzo's protégées, Miss Page Llanwelly. Miss Llanwelly, who has only recently returned from five years of study in France and Italy, has a gift for satire as well as art. The theme of her series of seven sketches was "Service in the Homes of the High and Mighty," and the sharp clean lines of her sketches, the skill of her portraiture, were as evident as a keen and biting wit.

Each separate sketch was accompanied by an equally satiric rhyme. *The Young Master,* for example, depicts a flamboyantly waistcoated young man with a watch chain stretched across a belly also stretched with culinary over-indulgence. He has a handsome face, disordered locks, and is obviously a little the worse for liquor. All this is conveyed in clear sharp strokes by the subtle skill of the artist. The rhyme of *The Young Master* declares rollickingly,

> *I'm the son of a lord*
> *And when I get bored*
> *I'm ripe for a lark,*
> *So when it grows dark*
> *Or even by day,*
> *I've got easy prey.*
> *The housemaid . . . the parlor*
> *maid . . . governess . . . cook . . .*
> *I'll take any one of them willing to be*
> *took!*

The Housemaid, a young, buxom, blowsy creature, is shown in two poses: one, down on her knees, shoulders hunched over, wearily scrubbing away at the kitchen floor . . . and then, lying on her back, a satisfied smirk on her plump face, her work-roughened hands in the act of lifting up her petticoats. The housemaid is saying:

AN UNFORGOTTEN LOVE

I make just a few pence
Down on my knees.
I can lie on my back
And there, at my ease,
Earn a month's wages
If the young master's pleased.

One of the more poignant sketches is of *The Sewing Woman*. This so-called woman is hardly more than a girl, a child even. She sits in the small sewing cell with the tools of her trade scattered all about her—an open box of threads ... a paper of pins ... darning materials ... socks with holes. . . . She is stitching at a piece of cloth, and in a face of Madonna-like loveliness are equally blended fatigue, fear and an awe-inspiring bewilderment. Her query is:

Me Dad can't support me
I've no place to go
I ain't got no savings
Me wages are low.
If the son of the house
Or the master or guest
Comes to this room
With a simple request,
What choice do I have,
If here I'm to bide,
But to pull up my skirts
And spread my legs wide?

The remaining four sketches all deal with the governess, or, as Miss Llanwelly—like our society—alternately styles her, the reduced gentlewoman. The governess's painful and ambiguous position in English society is introduced by Miss Llanwelly in two lines of gentle irony:

> *A governess works for the 'igh and the
> moighty
> Who demand she's a loidy but not
> hoity-toity!*

The artist–student's remarkable drawings then paint an incredibly vivid portrait of the English governess. In *The Reduced Gentlewoman, Interviewed,* we see a drab-looking creature, with a young-old face, suitably unpretentious in a dreary gown and a dark bonnet. She stands before a beautiful matron in a flowing tea gown, who is half-sitting half-reclining on a sofa, a fashion magazine to one side of her, a box of bonbons in her lap.

There are small skillful touches, a masculine power of perception and strength of detail that turn each simple sketch into a work of art . . . the careful darns in the gloves the governess is holding clenched between her hands, the mixture of boredom and contempt on the face of the matron, the languor and laziness of her pose . . . the timid, yet ingratiating smile on the face of the governess as she tries to sell herself.

The other three sketches in the series show *The Seduced Gentlewoman, The Governess Resists,* and *The Governess Is Dismissed,* along with other poignant rhymes, such as:

AN UNFORGOTTEN LOVE

Since she's the kind of gentlewoman
The gentry call "reduced,"
If the master tries seduction
She's supposed to be seduced!

Decidedly, Miss Llanwelly's is a talent well worth watching, and Paolo Lorenzo has once again proved that he is a master teacher as well as a master painter.

There was a copy of the *Art Journal* in a side pocket of Lord Vaile's crested carriage when Rupert handed Page into it for their third Saturday outing with his sisters. He indicated it as he took the seat opposite her.

"I wasn't sure you had seen this."

"I saw it." Page scowled.

He regarded her quizzically. "Two columns of praise from the highly critical Mr. Jowett. I thought you would be overjoyed."

"I was—till toward the end." She answered his unspoken question. "When he described," she quoted bitterly, "'my power of perception and strength of detail' as masculine."

"Ah."

"What do you mean, 'Ah'? Do you have any idea of the sheer arrogance and unconscious bigotry of such a statement? The *damned* stupidity? Oh, dear." She looked from left to right at Eliza and Emily, who were convulsed by giggles. "Pretend you didn't hear that, girls."

"I understand—in part, I think—your feelings,

but however ill expressed, the man did intend it as a compliment. It is no small thing that he thinks so highly of your work."

"The very fact he meant it for a compliment is what makes it all the more offensive. He is saying that something well done must necessarily be masculine. Look at it in reverse," she challenged him stoutly. "That paper on Mid-east archeological sites that you read at the Academy of Science lecture was extremely well received. The depth and accuracy of your research was applauded; both your work and your scientific findings were judged to be highly praiseworthy. How would you have liked it if, after all the adulation, it was *seriously* concluded that the merit of your work lay in its being *feminine,* or, in other words, equal to that done by a superior being, *woman?*"

There was no reply. Coming out of a happy state of bemusement, Rupert found Page, Eliza and Emily all waiting expectantly for an answer.

"I beg your pardon," he apologized to only one of the three. Then, "How did you know about my lecture?" he queried softly.

He saw the convulsive gulping inside her throat before she wet her lower lip with the very tip of her tongue and muttered something nearly inaudible about a notice in the *Times.*

"I don't believe the *Times* reviewed my lecture," observed Rupert judiciously.

"Several of the scientific journals did," mumbled Page.

"You looked it up. I am indeed flattered." But the sparkling triumph in his gray-green eyes, the touch of an exultant smile on his mouth belied the formal politeness of his words.

Goaded, Page flung at him, "So I went to the lecture." Her tone indicated another challenge. *So what?*

"I am happy to have awakened such scientific interest in you," Rupert said solemnly, while his eyes and mouth continued to smile and tell her, *As though I don't know you went to the lecture in order to see and hear me.*

Page hunched a shoulder to exclude him from the conversation.

"Where are we going today?" she inquired of her sisters. Last Saturday it had been the animals at Regent's Park Zoo and the week before the Monster Globe in the center of Leicester Square, both events followed by a sumptuous hotel tea.

"The new Crystal Palace at Sydenham," Eliza answered eagerly. "I can't wait to see the exhibition of extinged animals."

Emily bounced up and down. "And the sprouting fountains."

"Ex*tinct* animals, Eliza," Page corrected automatically. "And that's *spout*ing fountains, Emily."

They repeated the corrections together.

"Extinct."

"Spouting."

Emily added reproachfully, "If you'd come back to be our governess, we would *know*, besides everyone being happy."

"Everyone would be very happy," contributed Rupert, deciding to end his enforced state of isolation.

Page continued to ignore him.

"Let's recite poems, girls, to make the ride pass more quickly. Have you learned any new ones?"

Eliza obliged with a spirited, galloping rendition of "The Charge of the Light Brigade."

Her audience clapped heartily, and then Emily began,

> *"The Assyrian came down like the wolf*
> *on the fold*
> *And his . . . and his . . ."*

She giggled. "That's all I remember."

> *". . . and his cohorts were gleaming in*
> *purple and gold,"*

Page took it up.

> *"And the sheen of their spears was like*
> *stars on the sea*
> *When the blue waves roll nightly on*
> *deep Galilee."*

She smiled sheepishly. "That's all I remember."

"My turn then," said Rupert, and without further preliminaries, "Rise up, my love, my fair one, and come away," he recited in a quiet calm voice while his eyes blazed a message across at Page. "For, lo, the winter is past, the rain is over and gone, the flowers appear on the earth; the time of the singing of the birds is come, and the voice of the turtle is heard in our land."

"That's not a poem," protested Emily in disgust. "It doesn't even rhyme."

"It doesn't?" said Rupert with great good humor. "Well, how about this one then . . ."

> *"I'm the son of a lord,*
> *And when I get bored,*
> *I look for a wife,*
> *To add spice to my life."*

While his sisters laughed hilariously, he smiled at Page, who sat quite still, unaware that her arms were crossed protectively over her breast and her hands were clutching rather frantically at her shoulders.

"Page?"

She shook herself like someone coming up out of a dream. How could he know that she was thinking of a boy of thirteen who had seemed every bit as gentle as the present Rupert and yet been just as inflexible when he wanted to drive a point home? And *she* had been the one to knuckle in. . . :

"But I'm not seven years old anymore," Page said aloud suddenly, then began to laugh hysterically when they all stared!

Chapter Twenty-one

PAGE HAD RESOLUTELY DECLINED THREE INVITA-
tions in a row, but the last week in March she
received a note from Rupert informing her that
the Vailes were all removing to Derbyshire within a fortnight. "My sisters," he went on, "are
greatly desirous of seeing you one more time
before they leave London for so many months."

Prudently refraining from any mention of his
own desire, he added an invitation for her to join
them on a visit to Madame Tussaud's Waxwork
Show the first Saturday in April, to be followed
by their usual festive tea.

Having sent back a prim acceptance, Page

began counting off the slow-moving days that must pass until their meeting.

When the Saturday finally arrived, Eliza and Emily were so entranced by Madame's lifelike life-sized figures, and particularly with the Chamber of Horrors, which Page refused to enter, that the ex-governess and their brother were left frequently alone.

"I have missed you very much this last month," Rupert told her during their first interval of privacy.

In the second he elaborated this theme. "I shall miss you even more in the coming months. Unless, of course," he added offhandedly, "you choose to put an end to my misery by coming home with me . . . as my wife."

Page risked a fleeting upward glance. His tone might be light, even whimsical, but his face was set and serious.

"I'm sorry." She tried to sound as casual as he. "I can't."

"Can't—or won't?" When she didn't answer, he asked ironically, "Am I still unforgiven, Page?"

"It's not that. . . . At least," she added in a burst of honesty, "I don't think it's that anymore."

"I forgave *you* for holding up my family to ridicule," he pointed out mock-virtuously.

Page flushed slightly. "I didn't. Not the ones who counted . . . oh dear, I don't mean that the way it sounded. It was only your stepmother, who is hardly *au courant* with what goes on in the art world—not that I would care, anyway—and your brother Marcus, who doesn't mind. In fact," she finished defiantly, "he thought it extremely amusing."

"So he did, but how do you happen to know that?"

"Because I had dinner with him one evening, and he told me so."

"Did you indeed? How did that come about?"

"In the usual way. He invited me. You needn't worry," she said as a slight frown creased his forehead. "He was trying to advance *your* interests, not his own. He tells me"—she grinned mischievously—"that he's a reformed character as a result of my—er—lesson. He now only makes love to ladies who are both willing and in a position to say no."

"What Mark and his so-called ladies indulge in, Page, is not love but transient pleasure."

"Oh, I know that."

"I doubt it."

He touched her cheek lightly, fleetingly. "You and I, my darling, *would* make love." He paused. "Magnificently, I think."

Page felt a sudden rush of tears to her eyes. To her consternation, they overflowed and slipped down her cheeks. Rupert extended both index fingers to carefully blot them away; then, just as lovingly, he licked the salty wetness of her tears from off his fingertips.

Page's sudden impulse to throw herself into his willing arms and declare the world well lost for love was stopped by the eruption of Eliza and Emily into this emotion-charged scene.

"Rupert, Miss Llanwelly, you must come see the guillotine, it's splendid."

"And the torture instruments"—Emily shuddered pleasurably—"they're just gruesome."

"No, thank you," said Page firmly. "I can live without both the splendor and the gruesomeness."

Rupert, with a laughing backward look, unaware how close he had come to his heart's desire, obligingly went off with his sisters.

The farewells in front of Lorenzo's house a few hours later ended in general tearfulness, with both girls crying that they would miss her terribly, *horribly,* and Page, choked up, promising to write to them often and instructing both of them to write to her.

"Your brother will mail the letters for you, I'm sure."

Rupert nodded agreement.

"I'll be here in London for another six to eight weeks, and after that I'm going to Cornwall for the summer. I'll be staying at the St. Ives Day School."

"At school? You're going to teach?"

"No. It will be closed for the summer, but it's our home now. My mother and my young brother run it, and my father manages the gardens and

233

house repairs. It will be a vacation for all of us. I shall walk and climb and sun and swim and paint and picnic with my nephews and niece."

"It sounds heavenly," said Eliza enviously.

"You should have a good time, too. Perhaps Rup—your brother will take you digging in his cavern." They all looked at Rupert, who nodded again. "You might do some drawings of his fossils for him, Eliza." Eliza brightened. "But don't ever go swimming at the pond by yourselves, girls. Only if . . ."

"If Rupert is with them," said that gentleman resignedly. "I'll do that, too, I promise, and I also promise to tan their bottoms if they go alone."

While the girls were still giggling, Page gave them each a quick hug, whispered hastily, "I'll always be there if you need me," and bolted out of the carriage.

Rupert followed her in a less breakneck fashion and escorted her up the steps of Lorenzo's house.

"I, too, shall always be there if you need me, Page." He kissed first one of her hands and then the other. "*Au revoir, ma mie.*"

"Oh Rupert," Emily wailed, when he was back in the carriage and they were on their way home, "why didn't you make her come with us? Ow!" she shrieked as Eliza aimed a kick at her ankle.

Rupert's rigid features relaxed slightly. "Believe me," he said, "if I knew any way that I could have, most certainly I would have."

Silence reigned for the rest of the ride as Rupert looked somber, Emily subdued, and Eliza extremely thoughtful.

During their first weeks at Landsdowne Hall, Rupert tried to make life more cheerful for his sisters. No new governess had been hired, but the vicar's widowed daughter gave them lessons every morning. The music master came for Emily twice a month and a drawing master for Eliza twice a week.

On as many afternoons as their mother allowed, they dressed in their oldest clothes and went to the cavern with Rupert. He taught them the dull, careful process of proper digging and how to clean and label their finds in his laboratory.

Eliza, remembering Page's suggestion, secretly made a dozen pen and ink drawings of his best specimens and presented them to her brother all at once.

He was genuinely surprised and delighted. "These are marvelous, Eliza. Miss Llanwelly would be proud of you. When I write my book, I shall use them as illustrations, and your name will be listed as artist on the title page along with mine."

"Truly, Rupert?"

"Truly, Elizabeth."

Eliza sighed in ecstasy; a spasm of jealousy contorted Emily's face. Rupert, noticing this with an acumen he never would have experienced before the advent into all their lives of

Page Llanwelly, pulled at a strand of his younger sister's hair. "And Emily shall be mentioned in the acknowledgments," he said firmly, "with the author's grateful thanks for her invaluable help in digging at the cavern."

Two or three times a week Eliza and Emily lunched with him, picnic-style, at the cavern site. Afterward, they usually came back to the Dower House for tea. On a rainy afternoon toward the end of May, a sudden strong deluge kept them from going home at their usual time, and Rupert sent a message up to the Hall that they would stay with him for dinner. The carriage could be sent to get them later.

A gate-leg table was ordered set up in the library in front of a roaring fire lit to take the unusual chill out of the evening. Servants set out a dozen separate dishes on a long table and then departed.

"Help yourselves," their brother urged hospitably, seizing hold of his plate and proceeding toward this impromptu buffet.

"Oh, I wish we could always eat this way," Eliza said longingly later, when the table had been cleared and a bowl of fruit and an assortment of pastries brought in. She sighed for the contrast between this informality and the awful tedium of meal time at home.

After Rupert rang the bell for the removal of the pastries, with the dry comment that three apiece was more than enough for one night, his sisters walked around the room inspecting and admiring some of his Eastern treasures in their glass-enclosed cases . . . pottery, sculpture, coins and, lastly, a few paintings by Palestinian artists.

Emily, enraptured by a thousand-year-old vase, had no interest in the paintings on the wall until her sister gasped out, "Oh, my goodness, Emily, look."

Emily looked and uttered a high screech.

Rupert glanced up from the leather armchair where he sat, reading. "Oh, that," he said. "That's not from Palestine. A little girl—a very talented little girl gave it to me a long time ago."

"What was her name?"

"It's signed there . . . in the corner." He smiled reminiscently. "Her name was Vicky."

"But it's a drawing of Miss Llanwelly's bone!"

"I beg your pardon."

"It is, Rupert, it really is. The handkerchief . . . with the initials RV . . . and the fossil bone. She used to keep it on her writing table in a big shell box that one of her brothers made for her; she called it her treasure box. And after you qua—after she left us, Nellie found the whole thing—box and all—in the wastebasket. I think she threw it there in a—a—"

"Temper tantrum?" Rupert suggested coolly, despite the strange glitter of his eyes in his thin dark face and the cold clammy excitement churning up his insides, just as it did when he was on the verge of an exciting find.

"Well, no one ever tells us anything!" Emily

flared. "But if it *is* your bone, you must have hur her feelings badly!"

"If it *is* . . . you mean you took it from the basket?"

"Of course, we did."

"I shall go home with you when the carriage comes," Rupert rapped out decisively. "I would like to see—this bone. It might, of course, jus resemble the one I gave to Vicky."

"It's the same one," said Eliza with dignity pointing to the framed drawing. "I *recognize* it.'

Rupert recognized it, too, an hour later.

He hadn't thought of her in years, but he coul suddenly recall as though it were yesterday . . pressing it into her hands . . . the small curve bone with its one knobby end, swaddled in hi monogrammed handkerchief. His very first fos sil.

I want you to have it. . . . Now you'll have something that will make you remember me.

Good-bye, Vicky. . . . Take care of it for me.

And she *had* kept it and cherished it and remembered him through the years—my God, i must be all of fifteen!—until the day of their ugly quarrel.

But when had Vicky become Page? And why had she never reminded him of the past?

He set his mind furiously to think. She had lived with her aunt, an aunt who—good lord who had been governess to Diane, his stepmoth er. Supposedly, strong affection existed betweer the two, though it was Rupert's cynical conclu sion early in his father's marriage that Diane's greatest love was reserved for her own lovely self.

The fact was that Page now detested Lady Vaile. Had Diane, in some way, over the years, done the aunt an injury? Was the demand Page made for money because such a sum was owed?

He came out of his trance to see his two sisters staring at him with solemn, wide-eyed sympathy.

"Is it the same bone as the one Vicky drew?"

"Yes," he said huskily, "it is."

"Would you like to keep it, Rupert?" Emily asked him, almost motherly in her solicitude.

"Yes, thank you, I would."

"Is Page the same girl as Vicky?"

"I think so."

"When are you going to Cornwall?" asked Eliza shrewdly.

Rupert smiled with sudden radiance. "Tomorrow," he told them. "I shall leave as early as I can tomorrow. Bless you." He kissed and hugged them both, then administered a loving smack to each small bottom. "Remember, both of you," he warned, "stay away from the pond and the cavern till I get back."

Chapter Twenty-two

RUPERT VAILE STOOD IN THE RECEPTION PARLOR of St. Ives Day School, studying a portrait of three dark-eyed dark-haired boys that hung over the mantel. When Caroline Llanwelly walked in, his card in her hand, the years rolled back and he recognized her at once.

Though her hair had gone gray and her face was much more lined, still the years had been kind to her. She had gained in dignity and stature; there was serenity in her air and in her eye.

"Mr. Vaile, I am sorry," she said softly, "but Page is not here. We are expecting her next week."

"And you are. . . ?" Purposely he allowed his voice to trail off.

"I am Mrs. Llanwelly."

"Her mother?"

"Her mother," said Caroline with extra firmness.

He smiled. "I can't recall the name, I'm afraid, but the last time we met, you were her aunt *and* Diane—my stepmother's—governess."

"So you know that now, do you?" To his surprise, she seemed almost relieved. "Do sit down, Mr. Vaile," she urged him briskly. "You have had a long rail journey, and you look extremely weary. I have ordered some tea and sandwiches sent in. No, try the armchair over there; it's much more comfortable, and you can question me at your leisure."

He found himself responding instinctively to her refreshing candor and quietude and sank peacefully back into the oversized armchair she had indicated. Presently he accepted a plate of sandwiches she served him from the tray brought by a middle-aged maid and the cup of tea, to which, after a quick, questioning glance, she added sugar and milk.

What a restful woman! What a remarkable woman!

Unless he missed his guess, there was a history behind those tranquil eyes and the smile that suddenly made the Mona Lisa seem a simpering madam. The urgency of his mission seemed to melt away; he sat munching on a fish-and-lettuce sandwich and drank his tea while she sat across from him, quite obviously content to watch him and to wait.

She saw his eyes go back to the portrait over the mantel and spoke for the first time since she had invited him to be seated.

"Page painted it. My stepsons." There was pride, he noted, in both declarations.

"I thought I recognized her style, though, of course, this is more amateurish, but with flashes of brilliance." He got up and went over to the mantel to look at the painting again. "She makes them come alive. They're very alike . . . very Celt-looking."

"Like their father," she agreed, again proudly.

Rupert helped himself to another sandwich and resumed his seat. "Mr. Llanwelly is *their* father then, not Page's?" he asked her bluntly.

"It all depends on the way one looks at things, Mr. Vaile." The smile vanished, and she gave him a look as direct as his own. "I wed with Mr. Llanwelly when Page was a young child, in fact, just three weeks after her eighth birthday. She had never had a father. Her own was a soldier—an officer—who died in the service before she was born. She adored my Egan and badly wanted him to be her dad, and she wanted his name, too, so we let her take it. The thing wasn't done legally, you understand; it was just that we saw no harm in her calling herself Llanwelly, and for her a great deal of good."

A glimmer of the smile returned. "In a way, you might say Page adopted both of us. From the time she was four, she was . . . without a mother, so after a bit, instead of being Aunt Etti, I became mama."

"Why Page instead of Vicky?"

She laughed out loud, showing unusually sound teeth. "That's not as uncommon as you might think, Mr. Vaile. Half the children in this school decide to switch their names about a bit at one time or another. Haven't your sisters ever . . ."

"Come to think of it, they have," Rupert interrupted ruefully. "My sister Elizabeth was known as Lizzie until a few years ago, when she decided to be Eliza, and Emily used to be called Emmy."

It was only the next day when he was so fortunate as to be alone in the first-class carriage of the railcar on the early stages of his journey home, that he was to recall—as he went over every detail of his extraordinary visit—that she had not really answered that particular question. Not with an explanation or even a blank refusal, as when he asked about Page's dislike of Diane.

"I can't tell you that," she had said in her straightforward fashion. "It's for Page to answer, if she ever wants to. I can only say that, though I regret her feelings—it's my experience that hatred turns inward on the one who feels it rather than on the recipient—Page is . . . she has . . ." A note of caution crept into her voice. "Well, let us just say, there is some basis for the way she feels."

"You don't hate her yourself?"

"I? Hate Lady Vaile?" She shook her head. "Maybe once . . . long ago . . . I can hardly remember now. I only know it is years since I felt anything but sorry for her."

It seemed a strange statement to be coming from a neat but plainly dressed schoolmistress in a Cornish village of the elegant Lady Vaile, mistress of Landsdowne Hall; but looking at Page's mother, smiling again and serene, he had known it to be true.

He had prepared to take his leave after that, having, before he came to the school, reserved a room for the night in St. Ives.

Then he must take his dinner with them, Caroline Llanwelly insisted, if he didn't object to plain Cornish fare. It was a pity he wouldn't meet Patric who was on holiday in Wales, she went on, his acceptance taken as a matter of course; and Powys, he probably knew from Page, was ranching in Australia. But she would send a note by the butcher's boy to Cliff House, and Maura would bring the children early, and Egan could go down to the shore when the boats docked and bring Peter home with him straightaway.

"Though I warn you," she had laughed without apology, "his clothing will reek of fish . . . but his father can lend him a clean shirt. They are much of a size."

"I look forward to meeting Page's family."

"Page's family"—her eyes gleamed with merriment—"have quite looked forward to meeting you again, Mr. Vaile."

"Please call me Rupert. After all, I'm hoping to be your son-in-law one day."

"We're hoping the same thing, Rupert. It seems only fitting after all the time she's been in love with you."

"Then I was right. It wasn't just my imagination . . . or a wild conceit . . . that she came to Landsdowne after all those years . . . because of me."

"She didn't admit it when she left here, but yes, it *was* true. I knew, and so did her dad."

"But if she loves me, why won't she marry me?"

"You hurt her feelings badly; you hurt her pride even more. She had written to me that she was planning to tell you everything there was to tell just at the point when you jilted her and, in effect, threw her out of the house. . . . No, let's be honest," as Rupert uttered a strangled protest, "one day you were begging her to be your wife and the next handing her a check for money you thought she was trying to extort from Lady Vaile and giving her notice as your sisters' governess. If that's not jilting and throwing her out of the house, then it's as close as anything is like to be. Did you expect your later apologies to be accepted with instant delight? If you do, you don't know Page."

"I knew it would be an uphill struggle winning her back, but for God's sakes, it's been six months, and she was as adamant as ever about it the last time I saw her in London. She says it has nothing to do with what happened . . . it's just that she wants her freedom."

"Rubbish!" said Page's mother. "Married or a spinster, Page will always be free in spirit. You know that, don't you?"

He nodded.

"What's happened," she said thoughtfully, "is that you've been contrite a little too long and let her attitude harden. That's not good. It's up to you now, I think, Rupert."

"I don't want to walk roughshod over her to . . ."

"Don't worry. She won't ever let you do that."

"And I've been as humble as . . ."

"Perhaps the time for humility is past."

He grinned. "If I'm not to be either dom*ineering* or dom*inated*, what are the choices left me?"

"I have faith in you, Rupert Vaile," Caroline Llanwelly told him, her hand resting lightly on his shoulder. "You'll find a way."

As he journeyed back to Landsdowne, those words kept coming back to him, seeming more than ever both an accolade and an acknowledgment.

I have faith in you. . . .
You'll find a way. . . .

Chapter Twenty-three

Dear Miss Llanwelly,

I'm writing this at the Dower House, so no one will know. Rupert is at the cavern and his man Sean promised to mail it for me. I was scared if I left it for the post at home, my mother or father might read it. You're the only one I can write to because I don't know what to do, and you said you would always be there if I needed you. Well, I do. I need you awfully because something has happened I can't tell anyone else about, except Nellie, and she said it would be the best thing for me to tell you. I am in terrible trouble, so please come to

ne. *I will wait for you secretly every after-*
noon at the pond, starting in two days from
now.

I am sorry if this means you can't go to
Cornwall to your family as soon as you were
planning but I wouldn't ask if I truly didn't
need you.

> *Your loving pupil,*
> *Eliza Vaile*

Directing the coachman of the small shabby
brougham hired at the railway station to wait for
her, Page turned off the main road, climbed over
a fence and turned onto the Landsdowne property at the nearest point that would bring her to
the pond.

Eliza was sitting on the dock, fully dressed,
looking rather pale and pensive. Page felt a
sudden rush of protective love for her late-found
young sister.

"Eliza," she said softly, fearing to startle her.

Eliza turned her head, saw Page and promptly
burst into tears.

Page scrambled down onto the dock beside
her. "Tell me, Eliza," she urged.

"I thought you weren't coming," Eliza sobbed.
"I've waited every day for a week."

"I'm sorry it took so long, darling, but I had
already gone to Cornwall. Your letter was redi-
rected to me there. Now tell me what's wrong."

Eliza turned away. "I'm so—shamed," she

whispered. "In the beginning, it didn't seem s
bad, but now . . ."

"Eliza, are you—are you—?"

"I'm growing a baby inside me, Miss Llan
welly."

"Oh, my God!"

"You *are* ashamed of me, too. I told Nellie yo
would be."

"No, I'm not, darling." Page put her arm
around the weeping child. "Who was it, Eliza
How—?"

"The new drawing master."

"Oh, my God!" Page said again.

"He took me on long walks to find subjects t
draw, and mostly Emily came with us, but on
day she—he was so handsome, Miss Llanwelly
and he seemed to like me *so.* . . . I though
maybe I could get him to kiss me, only kiss me
So I told Emily to make some excuse to stay i
the gardens and I went alone with him to th
cavern. And he did kiss me, but then—bu
then—I was scared afterward, but he said not t
worry, nothing happened from just once. Only
a week later he told papa he had gotten a bette
position in a school in Bath . . . and then after ;
month. . . . It can happen from only once, can'
it, Miss Llanwelly?"

"I'm afraid so, Eliza, but are you *sure*
Sometimes . . ."

"I'm sure. Nellie took me to an old herb
woman she knows, and she looked at me an

hen gave me something to drink, only it didn't work and—"

"You mustn't take anything ever again!" Page cried, aghast. "Dear God, she could have harmed you."

"Nellie said there's a midwife she's heard of in the town who knows how to do—something— only she wants three guineas, and I don't have that much money, and besides I'm scared . . ."

"Eliza!" Page grasped her by the shoulders. "Promise me you won't go to any herb woman or midwife. Those women often don't know what they're doing; they could kill you. And with someone local, it would be bound to leak out . . . your life would be ruined. Now promise me."

"I promise," gasped Eliza, her eyes wide and frightened. "But Miss Llanwelly, what will I do?"

"I'll figure something out. I promise you."

They sat quietly for a while.

Page asked suddenly, "Is your brother home now?"

"Rupert. No, he went up to London a few days ago on business for my father. At least, that was his excuse. I think he really was hoping to see you before you left for Cornwall."

"Will he be there over the next few days?"

"I think so," Eliza said listlessly. "I heard papa tell his agent that he would not be back before Thursday next week."

"Very well," said Page. "Then you had better

get back to the house before someone comes looking for you and starts wondering what I'm doing here; I shall go straight up to London."

"You're not going to tell Rupert!"

"Not unless I absolutely have to, but"—Page lifted her chin, a decidedly martial light in her eyes—"I don't think I will have to. In any event you're not to worry. Everything will be all right, Eliza. I promised you, didn't I? Don't tell anyone else, and make sure Nellie doesn't say anything either."

They both stepped off the dock and onto the path. "You're not to lose heart if you don't hear from me right away. There may be—arrangements. That takes time." She squeezed Eliza's shoulder. "Trust me."

"I do, Miss Llanwelly."

Page looked into her pupil's shamed face. "I'm proud you turned to me, Eliza," she said.

Eliza put one finger in her mouth, burst into tears again and scuttled away. Page walked briskly along till she reached the main road where the brougham stood waiting.

"Back to the railway," she said curtly to the coachman.

The Vaile brothers were sharing the *Times* and enjoying a second cup of coffee when their London butler Sloan entered the breakfast parlor the next morning.

"Miss Llanwelly is here to see you, sir," he

announced to Rupert in a voice bristling with his own curiosity.

"Miss Llanwelly?" Marcus repeated incredulously.

Rupert put down his section of the newspaper and sat for several seconds, holding his cup in mid-air. Then, "Show her in here, please, Sloan," he directed quietly.

Both men were standing when Page entered the familiar sunny room. Under the watchful eye of Sloan, she shook hands with both of them but breathed a sigh of relief when the butler departed.

"Would you care to join us in a cup of coffee?" Rupert asked as calmly as though having a lost love drop in at breakfast time was an everyday event.

Page sat very erect in the chair he drew out for her. "Thank you, I would. As a matter of fact"—she glanced wistfully toward the sideboard—"I haven't had my own breakfast yet."

Concealing a smile behind his napkin, Marcus jumped up again. "Allow me," he said gallantly, went straight to the sideboard and started piling up a plate.

"Thank you," said Page again, even more fervently, as he set it down in front of her.

"If you will excuse me," said Marcus with unusual tact, "the Foreign Office calls."

Page bid him a grateful good-bye. The prospect of proposing to a man was difficult enough

without having his brother as witness. Just as i
would be easier to do on a full stomach than on
one that was sickeningly hollow. She attacked
her food with gusto.

When she had had her fill of eggs and coffee
muffins and marmalade, Page finally looked
straight at Rupert, who had been sitting across
from her, making small talk about the condition
of the queen, the country and the climate for the
benefit of a maid who came into the room a
intervals.

All during the trip from Derbyshire and in the
restless night's sleep under Lorenzo's roof, she
had planned all sorts of delicate ways to ap
proach him. To her own horror she heard hersel
pose the question with all the subtlety of a
Picadilly streetwalker soliciting a prospect.

"Do you still want to marry me?" she asked
Rupert bluntly.

There was the barest fraction of a pause
"Yes," said Rupert as the maid returned and
started clearing empty dishes from the side
board. "I do."

"I am willing then," Page said, bravely meet
ing his frowning look. She gulped. "Under cer
tain conditions."

Rupert rose and held out his hand to her.
"Shall we continue this discussion in the li
brary?"

Page rose, too, reluctantly accepting his arm.
She was afraid that he would feel her own arm

trembling, but if he did, he was kind enough to ignore it.

"And these conditions are?" he asked with such exquisite courtesy, she had no idea if he was feeling amused, abused or enraged.

She began to hedge a little. "It's this way," she explained. "Lorenzo was supposed to go to Florence for just the summer months, but he has decided he wants to stay on through the winter . . . and he wants me to come with him and study there . . . and I want to, of course. Only—"

"Only?" Rupert repeated unhelpfully.

"It would mean leaving you for almost—perhaps a year," she said barely above a whisper.

"And that, you discovered, would be a hard thing for you to do?"

"Yes."

"Now if I have this correctly . . . you are saying that you want both Lorenzo *and* me?"

Even as she turned a dull red, Page managed to utter another bald "Yes."

"Please state your conditions," said Rupert, crisp and businesslike.

"I will marry you now—any time—at once—if you will take me to Florence for our"—she swallowed hard—"for a long h-honey-m-moon. I-I could study with Lorenzo and you could study, too—there is lots of digging in Italy—and we could . . . could . . ."

"That doesn't sound unreasonable," Rupert

interrupted affably. "I am willing. Are *you* willing to have an immediate marriage? I would like to get a special license and do the thing as quickly as possible," he went on to explain, a gleam of humor in his eye, "before you change your mind again."

"I'm—that would suit me fine," Page mumbled with a strange feeling, half relieved, half apprehensive, that control had slipped from her hands to his.

"I will go at once to see about the license," said Rupert. "Shall I have the carriage take you back to Lorenzo's or will you go with me?"

Page put out her hand to stop him when he would have rung the bell. "There's one other thing I was thinking . . . we might . . . it might be a good idea to take Eliza with us."

"Eliza! Go with us!" Rupert stared at her. "Good God, you're serious! You really want to take my sister on our honeymoon?"

"It would be a m-marvelous op-opportunity for her," Page stammered. "To-to study and p-paint." She tried to pull herself together. "Your stepmother wouldn't let her go any other way . . . not alone, to school and to study, the way mine did. It's the one chance in a lifetime for her. She'd be very busy . . . not get too much in our way, if that's what you were worrying about," she went on boldly. "And Nellie would look after her, so . . ."

"Nellie?"

"Her maid."

"Her maid. Of course. How could I have forgotten the maid?"

"She's twenty," Page said hurriedly. "Old enough to chaperone Eliza and young enough to be a companion to her."

"My darling girl, I don't mean to complain. After all, an hour ago I was uncertain that I would ever get you back; now here we are planning a romantic journey to Italy. I do have some qualms, I must admit"—Page's fluttering heart settled a little more solidly in her breast for he sounded far more diverted than outraged—"I can't help wondering if we are going on a honeymoon or chaperoning a nursery."

"With Nellie to look out for her," whispered Page, "you and I will have much more time to be alone."

His face grew suddenly serious, but there was a tender smiling light in his eyes. "Do you very much want to be alone with me, Page?"

"I-I—"

"Look at me, Page."

Page looked at him. "I very much want to be alone with you," she told him, loud and clear.

Chapter Twenty-four

"PAGE LLANWELLY!" HER MOTHER CRIED, HORRI-
fied. "I must have heard you wrong."

Knowing full well this was only a manner of
speaking, Page nevertheless repeated with exaggerated care, "I said that Rupert had gotten
the special license and then gone to Derbyshire
to make the arrangements about his sister. He
expects to be here tomorrow morning and have
the wedding take place early in the afternoon so
that we can leave almost immediately for Plymouth where we take the ship for Italy. His man
Sean will meet us there with Eliza and her
maid."

She turned from her exasperated mother to

her open-mouthed father. "Will you speak to the minister, da?"

"Aye," said Egan, then shook his head doubtfully. "Are you sure you know what you're doing, lass?"

"Aye," Page said in turn. "I'm marrying a man who claims to want me more than anything else in life; and in doing so, I'm saving his—and *my* sister's reputation and future and providing a name as well as parents for her baby."

"I don't quarrel with your good intentions, lass," Egan told her gently. "But the way you're going about it . . ." He shook his head again. "I misdoubt he'll appreciate being informed of the circumstances afterward instead of before. The man might like a choice."

"I can't risk giving him a choice. *Eliza* can't afford any delay. That baby inside her is growing older by the day. As it is, it will be ticklish passing off the child as our own. We'll have to stay away at least a year . . ."

Caroline's face still registered strong displeasure. Page turned from her to Egan. "Please, da," she said coaxingly.

Never able to resist that tone, he took up the old fisherman's cap he still wore. "I'll be off to Mr. Morgan reet now."

Left alone together, Page stole a cautious look at Caroline. That lady, never one to mince words, even with her beloved daughter, told her forthrightly, "Page, you are doing wrong."

Page shrugged an impatient shoulder. "Oh,

mama, I have to do it, and it will all come out the same way in the end. He wants me, and he would want to protect Eliza and—"

"No man likes to be played for a fool—even to get his own way," Caroline retorted with energy. "If the child's a girl, it's no great matter. She'll just be another member of the family you'll no doubt have, seeing as how"—she eyed Page up and down very deliberately—"you're as mad for the man as you ever were. You can try to fool yourself about the why's of the marriage if you've a mind to. I know better. This way of getting him is a sop to your pride as much as a way to help your sister."

She ruthlessly overbore Page's blushing attempts to interrupt her. "But if it's a boy," she went on, "then the future heir will not be his own son and yours but the child of his half-blood sister's and a care-for-naught ne'er-do-well man's—and to that he might have strong objections."

As Page sat, suddenly struck silent, Caroline rose and moved toward the door. "I may as well save my breath to cool my porridge," she said dryly. "I know that mulish look of old, so I'd best send for Maura and start seeing to the luncheon."

"Luncheon?"

Caroline paused to bestow a brief forgiving kiss on one scarlet cheek and a pat on the hunched shoulder. "No daughter of mine is going to be married without a proper wedding neal!" she pronounced with dignity and sailed through the door.

Smiling in relief, Page jumped up and ran after her.

They were in the kitchen together drawing up lists when Maura arrived an hour later, carrying a tissue-wrapped bundle as tenderly as though it were a baby.

"My wedding gown," she announced, starting to pull the pins out of the tissue. "Hurry up, Page, and strip to your chemise so I can fit it on you. Thank God, we're not too different in height, but there'll be plenty of taking-in needed. You," she sighed mournfully, "are so much more slender than I was even before the bairns came."

"I wasn't planning on a formal gown," Page said hesitantly. "I thought perhaps one of my light dimities from Italy."

As though her sister-in-law hadn't spoken, Maura pulled out the last pin and held the gown in the air. From the fitted waist to the high-ruffled collar, the net bodice was covered in delicately worked lace. The tight long sleeves were made of the same lace and the petticoat, which formed the underskirt, was edged with it. The overskirt flowed out in layers of tulle.

"You'll look better in it than I did," Maura predicted gloomily, then turned toward Caroline and held up a matching confection of tulle and lace. "Won't the veil be just a dream on her, ma?"

"I don't want a bridal veil," Page protested.

"Yes, you do," Maura contradicted.

"You're going to be a bride, aren't you?" Caroline demanded.

They both advanced on Page, ruthlessly unbuttoning her buttons and divesting her of her morning dress, pulling and tugging her into the wedding gown, oohing and aahing and hushing her impatience.

"I knew how it would be," said Maura with her mouth full of pins. "You look a treat."

Page opened her mouth to protest. "Rupert will be so pleased," said her mother quietly. Page closed her mouth.

Rupert was more than pleased when Page, on Egan's arm, walked along the garden path of St. Ives Day School and joined hands with him before the minister underneath the arch formed by the fresh-cut branches of a great gnarled oak.

"You look beautiful," he whispered to her as the ceremony began. "I love you."

Page blinked rapidly. *I'm not going to cry*, she vowed and turned resolutely to face Mr. Morgan.

The short lovely service was over; they were man and wife. Page was held in his arms for a fleeting moment, then felt the light touch of his lips in a disappointingly brief, cool kiss.

She blinked again and, as though he could read her mind, Rupert whispered, "Later. We have our whole lives."

Peter and Patric were bussing her heartily; her nephews and nieces were clamoring to kiss her. Egan was shaking hands with Rupert, and Caroline was embracing her son-in-law far more warmly than he had embraced his new wife.

There was no time to be private, no time for further kisses or conversation until the wedding lunch was over, the tearful good-byes had been said.

As the heavy carriage with her luggage strapped on top bumped along the rutted path from the school over to the main road, Page hung halfway out the window, waving the lace-edged handkerchief from Eliza and Emily. Rupert had brought it with the message that it was "something new" to wear at her wedding.

When her family was no longer in sight, she sat back against the cushions and Rupert leaned across her to close the window, shutting out the choking dust of the road.

The new-made husband and wife looked at each other, Page's smile a bit tentative, Rupert's so transparently pleased, so patently possessive, that her legs shook against her modest crinoline and the lace jabot of her blouse, foaming over the peach jacket of a smart Italian traveling costume, was stirred by her thumping heartbeats.

She was not nearly so afraid of the demands that Rupert would presently make on her as she was of the confession about Eliza that, sooner or later, would have to be made to him. Egan's warning and Caroline's prediction sounded in her ears with an ominous immediacy she had dismissed—too arrogantly, she now realized—the day before.

As her eyes grew wider and more frightened, Rupert said softly, "I think you were disappointed that I chose to wait till now for the kind of kiss I really longed to give you." His fingers—long, strong, browned—caressed her chin and tipped her face up to his.

"Shall we try again, Page?"

Without waiting for an answer, his mouth claimed hers with all the passion that had been missing before, the ardor his slightest touch stirred in her and the love that had been there since the very beginning.

Page burst into tears.

Rupert put her away from him, his eyebrows raised in comical distress.

"I didn't realize I was quite that much out of practice," he said, both his hands covering hers as they lay trembling in her lap.

"Oh no, you're not—I'm not—it's not—"

After waiting a moment to hear if anything sensible would follow these stumbling incoherencies, "You're just tired," Rupert said soothingly. This time his hands didn't hold or press or grip any portion of her but merely patted her shoulders in the kindly way of a parent comforting a fractious child. "Too much has happened in too short a time."

He whisked the lace handkerchief from be-

eath her hands and used it lightly, still pater-
ally, to blot away her tears.

"Shall we remove your bonnet, Page?" Again,
without waiting for an answer, he proceeded to
o so.

"Wh-what f-for?"

"It's decidedly fetching but very much in the
vay."

Her face flooded with color; her breathing
uickened. Half-unconsciously, as he untied the
legant bow made by Maura's clever fingers not
nany minutes before, Page leaned toward him,
er lips moist and full and willing.

Rupert set the bonnet down on the seat beside
im and ignored the obvious invitation of her
nouth.

"There, that's better," he said with apparent
atisfaction. "Now you can put your head on my
houlder and rest."

"R-rest?"

"Till we get to Plymouth," he said sympatheti-
ally. "So much has happened in the last few
ays, I doubt if you have had your proper sleep.
Jo wonder you're so ner—weary."

The tactful substitute word came too late to
niss giving offense. Page's eyes flashed. "I do
ot get nervous!"

"Of course not. You are merely over-fatigued.
)ne doesn't get married every day, after all—
specially not on such short notice." He yawned.
Truth to tell, I'm a bit weary myself. So

many arrangements . . . and all that travelin
around. . . ."

He drew her into his arms and pressed he
head down on his shoulder. It felt so comfor
able, so comforting, that her first impulse t
resist melted away, and instead, she bent he
legs up and snuggled against his hardened bod
like a kitten; she was purring like one, too.

Presently, she fell asleep, and not too man
minutes later, so did he.

He awoke, instantly alert, when the carriag
came to a stop. Page slept on, her head no longe
on his shoulder but heavy against his side. Sh
lay half across his lap, both her arms aroun
him, her hands clutching at the back of hi
jacket as though he were her strength and he
sanctuary.

He sat a moment, savoring that convictior
then shook her gently. "Page, wake up. We are a
Plymouth."

Page slowly struggled out of a deep sleep to th
sound of Rupert's voice. "Smell the sea, da
ling," he said as she lifted herself. "And look . .
there is our honeymoon ship."

Chapter Twenty-five

UNUSED TO THE LUXURY OF FIRST-CLASS TRAVEL, 'age was somewhat overwhelmed by the splendor of their good-sized cabin with the even more ommodious sitting room that adjoined it. There vere three vases of flowers that carried brief, musing messages of good will from Marcus nd two baskets of fruit containing Lord Vaile's ard.

Rupert suggested they go up on deck while heir bags were being unpacked.

"I think I should see your sister first." Eliza, 'age reflected, would surely need reassurance.

"I checked with the purser. Sean has not rrived yet."

"But we sail in just over an hour."

"He knows what time they must be here. [I]t was a long journey." Rupert put an arm light[ly] around her. "Don't worry. Sean has never faile[d] me. Do you know," he asked after a momen[t] "that you are sniffing that not-altogether-de[-] lightful aroma with much more pleasure tha[n] you smelled your flowers?"

For the first time since their vows had bee[n] spoken, Page gave him a natural smile. "Flow[-] ers may be fragrant, but fish-scented sea wate[r] is positively heavenly."

"So are you."

"Huh?"

"Positively heavenly."

Page looked resolutely out at the broad gra[y] expanse of the Channel. "Th-thank you."

"I ordered dinner for two served in the cabi[n] after we set sail," Rupert mentioned after anot[h-] er slight pause.

"B-but w-wouldn't—w-won't that be rude [to] Eliza?" Page stammered out.

"I think Eliza is old enough to appreciate tha[t] tonight we would like to be alone together."

Page blushed madly. "Of c-c-course," she stu[t-] tered. "I just thought . . ." After a short inne[r] struggle, she managed to pull herself togethe[r] "The first-class dining room is bound to be quit[e] sumptuous," she said in an airy manner.

"No doubt . . . and I will be most happy to se[e] it," Rupert agreed politely, "but tomorrow, n[ot] on our wedding night."

Page swallowed. "I think I should go back to
ur cabin and supervise the unpacking."

"Do you mind if I stay up on deck and wait for
ean?"

"No, no, of course not; I think you should,"
age declared fervently, picked up her skirts
nd fled.

Forty minutes later, when Rupert entered so
uietly she did not hear him, the unpacking
as done, the maid was gone, and Page was
neeling on a chair and staring out of a port-
ole.

She whirled around and jumped to her feet
hen he said her name. "Sean is here," Rupert
nnounced.

"Oh, thank goodness. I was beginning to be
oncerned." She came toward him eagerly.
What cabin is she in?"

"Page, she—"

"I promise not to be away too long." She
miled placatingly. "I just want to make sure
hat she and Nellie are settled in and—"

"Page, listen to me." His hands on her shoul-
ers, even more than his voice, commanded her
tention. "Sean is alone."

"Eliza—?"

"Eliza did not come."

I am not going to faint, Page told herself. *I
ever faint. Never ever.*

"Oh my God, what happened?" she said aloud.

Rupert was regarding her quizzically. "Is it
eally such a tragedy if she comes a few months

later?" he asked. "We do," he reminded her wi
gentle irony, "have each other."

Page asked him, dry-mouthed, "*Is* she comi
a few months later?"

"If we still want her, my father will send h
with Nellie and a courier to take care of the
both on the journey."

"But why"—Page tried to sound nonchalant
"why did he change what seemed an ideal trav
arrangement . . . I mean, her coming now wi
us?"

"I'm afraid," said Rupert, wryly, apologeti
"my father—surprising as it may seem to you
tends to be rather romantic. On further deliber
tion, after my hurried visit home, he decided
would be unfair to burden a newlywed coup
with the care of a young girl and her attendar
He felt—erroneously, it would seem—that v
would rather be alone for a period and that, if v
still wished, Eliza could join us later."

Page stood rooted to the spot, wanting to te
her husband that his father's romantic decisi
was far from erroneous, that the delay in Eliza
arrival was *not* a tragedy; above all, wishing
declare that she *would* far rather be alone wi
him for a time. Unfortunately, her tong
seemed to be as paralyzed as the rest of her a
she could only stare at him in speechless, glaz
eyed fright.

What would become of Eliza now, and wh
would become of Rupert later when he fou
out?

And why, suddenly, did her relationship with upert seem so complicated simply because liza was not with them?

Nothing really had changed, Page told herself esperately. If Eliza had come, as planned, Rubert and she would still be dining alone together the intimacy of their own cabin tonight. He ight discard his more formal clothes for the omfort of a dressing gown and expect her to ear one of her filmy *chemises de nuit* and a egligee. There would be wine with their diner, champagne perhaps; and after the table as cleared and the remains of their meal emoved . . . then they would be truly alone . . .

Rupert would expect to take her to bed with im. Instinctively, she knew that he would reove her robe and gown as well as his own. The upert she knew and had fallen in love with ould want bare skin against bare skin.

She closed her eyes dizzily . . . he would make ve to her skillfully, urgently, ardently, as she ad wanted him to do for so long, so long. . . .

Why then was she so frightened of *it* and of im—only because Eliza was not now with em?

She opened her eyes to find Rupert holding out n envelope, looking at her expectantly.

He must have said something or asked someing.

"I beg your pardon."

"I said," Rupert repeated patiently, "that liza sent you a letter."

Page almost grabbed the envelope from h
hand. She slit it open with a fingernail and,
the pretext of needing more light, turned aw
from him toward the nearest porthole as sl
spread open the single page. It trembled in b
hand as she read.

Dear, dear Page,

*I can call you Page now, can't I, instead
that awful formal Miss Llanwelly since you a
married to Rupert and truly my sister?*

*Don't be worried about me because I won't
coming to Italy until September or October.
least, I'll come then if you and Rupert stay
so long and still want me. I was the one wl
gave papa the idea that it would be in bett
taste not to interfere with your honeymoon.
course, I didn't tell him the reason I was wi
ing to do it before no longer exists.*

*I am fine, Page. Really fine. Do you unde
stand what I mean? That problem we though
had, I don't have; it was all a mistake,
there's no hurry for me to come to Italy, eve
though I can hardly wait. Maybe, so long
there's not that problem, you wouldn't mi
having Emily come there with me. Would you
It would be such fun, and we would have ea
other when you two honeymooners want to
alone.*

*I'm so happy about everything, Page, and
glad you're my real-true sister. I love you mo*

*han anyone except Emily and Rupert, and I
hank you with all my heart anyway.*

*Your loving sister,
Elizabeth Vaile*

As Eliza's letter dropped from her nerveless
ingers to the floor, Page stared sightlessly out of
he porthole window. When her eyes began to
ocus again and her wits to function, she be-
:ame conscious of the engines humming be-
leath her feet and the slap of the water against
he ship's side. They were on their way.

England, with a non-pregnant Eliza in it, lay
ehind them; Italy lay ahead. And she was here
llone, starting her honeymoon with the man she
oved. . . . *Oh, I love him, all right; as usual,
nama was right. The only one I fooled for even
l moment was myself,* thought Page with pain-
ul clarity.

The man she loved would expect her any
noment now to be loving and ardent and enrap-
ured, and God knows it would be wondrously
:asy to forget the past and be all those things . . .
vondrously easy . . . and impossible!

Her own nature made it unendurable for there
o be a marriage, let alone an unrestrained
nating, without the truth, the whole truth being
)ared between them.

She would enjoy telling him that she was little
Ticky, his young playmate of long ago. Undoubt-
:dly, that revelation would only intrigue him.

Her being his stepmother's daughter—as Caroline had long ago pointed out—reflected discredit not on her but on Lady Vaile; and Rupert need never shame his father with such knowledge.

The matter of Eliza . . . therein lay the rub . . . how would he feel when he learned that she had married him, intending to palm off his half-sister's bastard as his own child without giving *him* the right, let alone the chance to say yes or no?

The coward's voice within her offered temptation. *He need never know*. Certainly, Eliza would not betray her.

The Page who had been brought up by Caroline Llanwelly pushed temptation away. *If our marriage is to be of consequence, then it can't begin with a lie*.

Rupert was standing in front of her; she had not even heard his approach. "Page," he was saying softly. She had no idea how many times he had spoken her name.

"What is it, my love?" he asked her with such adoring gentleness, her eyes filled up and her knees grew weak.

He could be so tender, so loving, so—she shuddered, remembering the painful swiftness with which she had been handed a handsome check, the implacable coldness with which she had been given notice—so merciless, so unyielding when his high standards were not met.

She suddenly knew if she lost him, especially before she even had him, then the whole meaning

ing of her life would be lost, too. Oh, she would survive, she would go on—she was no silly, simpering weakling to pine away for love. Still, life without Rupert would be but a poor pale imitation of the gloriously fulfilling life they could live together.

She found herself gasping for breath at this horribly unwelcome knowledge. Her knees buckled under her, and she looked wildly about. The rushing heaving movement of the Channel waters seemed to be repeating their motion inside her own churning stomach and spinning head.

As he stepped forward, startled by the look of abject terror on her face, Page managed to stagger past him and reach the wash basin. "Go away," she wailed pitifully. "P-p-please g-go a-way."

Chapter Twenty-six

A SYMPATHETIC STEWARDESS, HAVING WASHED her face with cool water and provided a foul-tasting drink she claimed would help, had removed the embarrassing evidence of Page's frailty.

"You have only to ring if madame needs anything else," she offered eagerly as she stood at the cabin door, fingering a crisp new bank note just tucked into her uniform pocket.

"I shall do everything else that madame requires," smiled Rupert, attempting to speed her on her way.

Remembering suddenly that they were honeymooners—the ship's crew could always tell—

he stewardess smiled another China-white mile and closed the door behind her.

Page, lying limply on top of the coverlet, not oo aware of what was going on around her, ound herself being unbuckled, unbuttoned and undressed with a speed and competence both urprising and significant when the unbuckler, unbuttoner and undresser proved to be her husband.

Before her embarrassment could reach full eak, a nightgown was slipped over her head and her arms pulled through the sleeves. She vas briefly hoisted up, popped underneath the covers, and the nightgown tucked with the greatest modesty about her ankles.

He could barely hear her murmur as he took he pins out of her hair and scattered it loose against the pillows. "You do—this—much—too vell."

"You sound very wifely." Rupert grinned. "Jealous, my sweet?"

"Not," Page said with dignity, "of your past."

"Point taken, Mrs. Vaile."

"Though I gather that it has been . . . that you have been . . ."

"The better to please *you*, my love," Rupert reminded her virtuously.

Page's voice became a little less enfeebled. "Shall you say the same if *I* am not without experience?"

"It wouldn't be fair for me to answer that as hough I believed that you might be," Rupert answered quite seriously. "I know that you have been kissed and romanced before me—incredible if you hadn't been after all those years in France and Italy—but I also know that you are a virgin."

Page tried to sit up, found herself too weak and sank back, demanding tartly, "How *can* you know?"

"If I am wrong, the proof will soon be forthcoming, my dear . . ." Then, as every inch of skin not covered by the nightgown was colored a rich, hot red, he added without subtlety, "but not tonight."

Her eyes grew enormous with gratitude. She said, "Oh, thank you," in tones so fervently thankful his own brows raised in slightly pained protest.

"You needn't sound quite so much as though you had been spared a terrible ordeal," Rupert reproached her. "I merely do not wish to take advantage of a tired and ailing wife." His voice turned silky. "There would be no pleasure in it for either of us if I did. By the way, I thought you once told me that you never get seasickness?"

"Seasick . . . oh!"

Page's eyes closed while her mind worked furiously. Seasickness. Of course. What more natural than thinking she was seasick? A much more normal assumption than that she had been overcome by a sudden violent response to a week of emotion, strong stress and worry, to

278

say nothing of a hasty wedding followed by more stress, emotion, shame, regret and sheer fright!

Seasickness. Oh, thank you, God, she prayed with unwonted humility. A whole long night's reprieve.

"I boasted too soon," she confessed ashamedly to Rupert. "I was most vilely overcome."

"I know, my dear," said Rupert, patting her hand. "That's why I cancelled our private dinner." With one finger, he stroked some of the silken strands clinging damply to her forehead. "Don't worry about me," he told her softly. "I shall take my meal in the public dining room after all. I shan't mind, I promise you. You try and get some rest, love, while I change to evening wear."

He smiled at her very lovingly; Page's smile was a weak imitation.

She lay with eyes closed through the sounds of his change in clothing. Half an hour before she could have asked for no greater boon than to be alone with no demands made on her other than to rest and recruit her strength.

She had gotten all she claimed to want, and yet—a few weak, silly tears trickled from her eyes, and she dashed them away impatiently with the back of her hand.

"Page?"

She opened her eyes. He looked positively dashing in his evening frock coat of navy blue with a dazzlingly white starched and ruffled dress shirt and a satin waistcoat. She looked him over from head to foot. There was a sapphire ring on his hand that she had never seen him wear before, and his shirt cuffs contained links of ancient beaten gold that no doubt came from the Holy Land.

"I'm going now. Will you be all right?"

"Of course."

She closed her eyes again and felt the brief cool touch of his lips against her forehead—more impersonal even than their after-wedding kiss. The door closed. Page sat up, hugging her knees and swearing.

That browned face, that bearing . . . he was magnificent, and he was *hers,* damn it, and here she was, forced to sit alone on her wedding night while he undoubtedly would not be alone in the first-class dining room. The women would be all over him till *Mrs.* Vaile was in shape to assert prior claims!

And, worst of all . . . "Damn, damn, damn," she gritted out, as her poor stomach rumbled indelicately aloud.

She had hardly eaten a bit of breakfast or her wedding luncheon. She hadn't had a bite since either. Now that there was a reprieve from the confession that must come . . . the lovemaking to be . . . her normal appetite—for food, at least —had returned in one great overwhelming wave.

"I'm hungry," moaned Page to the empty

om. Then she smacked her pillows viciously
d tried to settle down.

Twenty minutes later she was still wide
vake, still hungry. "Oh, God, I'm staaar-ving,"
e wailed pitifully just as the door opened and
e stewardess tiptoed in.

She eyed Page's flushed face and thrashing
dy with some trepidation.

"Mrs. Vaile, are you ill again?"

Immediately Page resumed her wilting violet
se.

"Just a little weak," she said in failing ac-
nts.

"Your husband asked me to see if there was
ything you needed, and you're not to worry
out him, he's doing fine." She beamed. "Such
thoughtful man."

"Isn't he just?" Page muttered below her
eath. Then, "Do you know what he's eating?"
e couldn't resist asking aloud.

"Well, I'm not sure." The stewardess hesi-
ted. "There's so much choice . . . but I think
e specialty tonight is fillets of veal in a wine
uce."

Page swallowed. "Could—could you get me
me tea? I—it would help settle my stomach."

"Yes, of course, Mrs. Vaile. Anything else?"

Page hesitated. She longed to say, *some bread
nd butter*. Perhaps even, *a morsel of chicken*.
ut if she did and Rupert found out . . . And this
othy creature who seemed so enamoured of
im couldn't be trusted not to tell him.

"I can't manage anything except the tea, I
afraid," she declared wanly.

Five minutes later, while waiting for her te
she was struck by a brilliant inspiration a
went tearing into the sitting room, past t
splendor of Marcus's flowers and straight to t
baskets of fruit sent by Lord Vaile.

"Oh, thank God! And thank *you*, Lord Vai
forever and ever, amen," she breathed. A
then, "For this I shall be the best daughter-i
law any father ever dreamed of having," s
vowed.

She selected two peaches, two nectarines a
a small scoop of cherries before coming upon t
real treasure trove of the basket . . . a sm
packet of biscuits and a fat round jar of goos
berry preserves! After she laid out all the
edibles on the blotter of the writing desk tuck
in a far corner of the sitting room, Page pr
ceeded to rearrange the contents of the basket
that her depredations on it would not be easi
noticed.

Then she fled back to her berth. Just in tim
too. In another few minutes the stewardess h
arrived with her tea.

"Just leave it on the nightstand," Page utter
faintly to the stewardess. "And I would rath
not be disturbed again tonight, please. I thi
after I have my tea, I will be able to sleep."

The moment she was alone, she leaped
again, seized hold of the tea tray and sped ba
to the sitting room, where she sat at the de

ith a huge linen cloth tied under her chin to
otect her nightgown. She wrenched open the
r of preserves and heaped huge spoonfuls of
m onto half a dozen of the biscuits, then
oured a cup of tea. Having finished this
rst course—which only whetted her appe-
te—she cut up a peach in her teacup, added
ome milk and sugar, and greedily gobbled it
own. This dish proved so delightful, she de-
ided to repeat it—and did. By the time she
ad drunk her second cup of tea and eaten
e remainder of the biscuits and jam, all the
herries and one plum, she was contentedly re-
lete.

She restored the lone leftover plum to the
asket, cleared away all traces of her clandes-
ne feast, and returned the tea tray to her
edstand.

Curled up against her pillows again, she
tarted making plans. Perhaps in the morning,
fter her first night's sound sleep in a week, she
ight feel less awkward, more able to deal with
situation that called for every ounce of brains,
f tact, of—

Full of optimistic plans for approaching her
usband with cunning as well as courage, hon-
sty without undue humility, love without too
uch lowering of her crest . . . the new Mrs.
aile fell asleep.

She did not hear her husband's quiet entrance
r his rueful sigh as he gazed down on his
leeping wife. She missed the rueful smile with

which he straightened her blankets and pr
ceeded to the sitting room, where he spent tl
night on the sofa.

For all that she passed the more quiet ar
satisfying night of the two, Page was the last
awake. Her husband was standing over he
fully dressed in light gray flannel trousers and
fawn blazer, a striped tie and an air of disgu
ing bonhomie.

His voice could not have been more polit
more punctilious, more over-hearty and mo
unconcerned if they had been ten years marrie

Page, who had just yawned indelicate!
stretched deliciously and opened her mouth
answer, "Marvelous," found herself with not
ing to say at all.

Rupert seemed not to notice.

"I was just going to breakfast," he announce
cheerfully. "I hadn't planned to disturb you as
didn't think you would want to eat. I must sa
this sea air whets *my* appetite."

His booming laugh sounded much too loud
the small space. Page winced. Insensitive brut

She debated mentioning that she felt we
enough to have breakfast with him. In the cr
cial moment while she tried to make up h
mind, Rupert informed her jovially, "You
never guess who I met in the dining room la
night."

Page performed *this* wifely obligation,
least. "Who did you meet?" she asked dutifull

"Charley Witherspoon."

"Charley Witherspoon," Page repeated blankly. Who the devil was Charley Witherspoon?

"Yes, good old Charley Witherspoon. We were at Eton together. I haven't seen him for donkey's years. He's married, too, now . . . to a daughter of old Lord Beasley. You know, the one they used to call the preacher lord. His life's work was the reform of Magdalenes. I understand Charley's wife is continuing it as a memorial to him. She thought you might be interested in aiding her Reformation Society, or some such group, for the support of fallen women. Anyhow, I'm having breakfast with them. Do you think you might be up to joining us?"

"M-most definitely not." Shuddering at the prospect of breakfast with the reforming Mrs. Witherspoon, Page sank back against her pillows. "I—I still f-feel a little queasy," she told him pathetically.

"My poor darling," said Rupert and kissed her perfunctorily on the forehead. "Ring for the stewardess if you need anything."

Ten seconds after the door closed behind him, it opened again. "I'll promenade on the deck for a bit after breakfast. Then I'll probably be in the card room. You can send for me any time you want, my dear."

"Thank you, Rupert," she made herself say sweetly.

My dear. My dear! If he called her *my dear* just one more time in that unctuous voice, she would throw something at him. Before this trav-

esty of a honeymoon it had been *darling a*
dearest and *my sweet*.

"Bastard!" she addressed the closed door.
promptly opened again.

"I beg your pardon, madame," said a pain
voice—the stewardess arriving with her mor
ing tea tray.

"I said 'Blast it!'" Page told this barefaced
with a plaintive smile. "How would *you* like
have seasickness on your honeymoon?" she fi
ished pitifully.

Chapter Twenty-seven

SHE HAD BREAKFASTED ON SOME SCOTTISH shortbread found in the second basket of fruit, lavishly spreading it with the remainder of the gooseberry preserves, also an assortment of peaches, plums, nectarines and grapes and, of course, two cups of tea.

By lunch time, when Rupert breezed in to inquire after her well-being, she felt genuinely queasy and told him so. After a very few words of solicitude, he breezed out again. She had obviously, she decided bitterly, taken unto herself a husband who stayed as far away as he could from female illness.

Page was left feeling more than slightly pan
icky. Were the fates punishing her with a genu
ine attack of seasickness? It was a while befor
it occurred to her that such a surfeit of fruit fo
two meals in a row might produce much th
same symptoms. She decided to omit luncheo
except for the inevitable tea.

By dinner time she was commencing to b
hungry again. She was also bored, lonely an
feeling as much a prisoner as though an iro
grill kept her within the cabin.

They had been married at least thirty hour
and the only time she had been alone with he
husband—both in the carriage and on the ship-
she had spent sleeping. They had hardly ex
changed more than a dozen sentences, let alon
—let alone—

She went over to the wardrobe and bega
examining negligees. The silvery gray chiffo
had a beautiful matching gown. On the othe
hand, it was not quite as enticingly feminine a
the low-cut fitted cream silk. Or was the crean
silk too obvious? The small, spring-flowere
dimity with its square-necked ruched bodice an
the bow ties at its tight waist was, perhaps, mon
subtly seductive . . .

Did she want to be subtle? Did she want to b
seductive? Did she want to be both or neither?

Above all, was she ready to suggest that Ru
pert and she have the postponed wedding-nigh
supper for two in the privacy of their own qua
ters?

Recklessly, she removed the cream silk robe from its hanger and rummaged in her drawers for the nightgown that would best blend with it.

Let's be obvious, lass, she told herself. *You know what you want; it's time that he knew, too.*

They would eat by candlelight, and she would ask him to order champagne. Lots and lots of champagne.

There was no more potent beverage when it came to untying the tongue.

Full of good food—solid food like veal or beef or lamb, garden vegetables, potatoes, anything but fruit—awash with champagne, she could tell him all. She *would* tell him all.

And when that was behind them, with the same delicious skill he had shown the night before in divesting her of her clothes, he would remove the fitted dressing gown and then the silk nightgown, the satin slippers with the jeweled buckles, and the gold chain around her neck that nestled provocatively just where the separation of her breasts began . . .

And then—and then—

Aroused by her own erotic thoughts, she leaned against the wardrobe in breathless, dizzy anticipation, which Rupert, entering quietly, saw and misinterpreted completely.

He leaped to put an arm around her and lead her back to her berth. "You shouldn't have gotten out of bed, you're obviously not well enough," he scolded gently. "Why didn't you

ring for the stewardess if you wanted some
thing?"

Page lifted her still-flushed face to his as h
pushed her under the covers.

"But I—but I—"

"You're a little fevered, I think," worried R
pert, his hand on her forehead. "I had so hope
you would feel well enough to have dinner wit
me tonight. The Witherspoons agreed to shar
my table, and they are so anxious to meet yo
They will be greatly disappointed that you ar
still unwell."

So much for candlelight, champagne and con
fession, Page reflected grimly, resisting th
childish urge to throw herself on his chest an
weep with disappointment. Instead, since slo
starvation sounded preferable to the Wither
spoons, she stared with something akin to ha
tred at this insufferable boor who was he
husband, yet appeared perfectly contented t
forego a husband's privileges.

"Perhaps I should send for the ship's doctor."

"No!" said Page crossly. "I just want to be le
alone."

"Certainly, my dear," said Rupert soothingly
"I understand."

To her fury, he whistled quite cheerfully as h
washed and dressed in his dinner clothes. Yo
unfeeling monster! Page mouthed silently t
her beloved while the slow tears dripped dow
onto her pillow.

She pretended to be asleep when he left, the

slowly counted off five minutes on the little traveling clock he had thoughtfully provided for her bedstand before she rang vigorously for the stewardess.

When that poor harassed woman arrived, Page was standing in front of the mirror brushing out her hair. She wore a pale yellow lawn nightgown and the spring-flowered dimity robe with its ruched bodice and the bow ties at the fitted waist, her Roman-style gold velvet slippers with the criss-cross cords around her ankles.

"I would like to have dinner served to me in my sitting room," Page said as haughtily as though the stewardess rather than her husband was the object of her displeasure.

"Yes, ma'am, certainly, what can I order for you?"

"Baby lamb chops, three of them, I think," said Page, her mouth watering at the very thought. Suddenly she became herself again. "Potatoes—mashed or baked or boiled, I don't care what kind, but lots and lots of them. Two green vegetables and a basket full of bread. Nice thick *chunks* of bread, mind, not those thin skimpy slices."

"Coffee, madame, and perhaps a strawberry tart or the chef's special apple pie?"

Page shuddered. "Heaven forbid! Nothing with fruit. And no coffee." She had a sudden inspiration. "I know. A bottle of champagne."

"Any particular champagne?"

"Any at all," Mrs. Rupert Vaile answered airi-

ly, though it was Page Llanwelly who added
with belated caution, "Mind you, not too dear."

Half an hour later, as Page sat on the sofa in
the sitting room, reading Jane Austen's *Emma*, a
tap on the door heralded the arrival of a white-
jacketed steward wheeling in her dinner table. A
waiter just behind him carried a bucket with her
champagne.

The table was ceremoniously set in the center
of the room and a straight-backed chair placed
in front of it.

"Shall I open the champagne immediately
madam?"

"Please," said Page, smiling impartially at the
two of them, "and then you may both go. I prefer
to serve myself."

"Certainly, madam."

The cork was removed, a small amount
poured and submitted for her approval.

"Delicious," said Page after one quick sip,
anxious only to get rid of them.

She took an ecstatic spin around the room
after they had gone, then sat down at the table
and lifted the silver cover from off her dinner
plate.

She sniffed joyfully at the baby lamb chops in
their silly frilly little paper jackets ... but all
the better to take them into her hands instead of
using knife and fork. She devoured the first one
voraciously, then turned her attention to the
asparagus, the garden peas, the big round baked
potato dripping with butter.

Halfway through the meal, she spread her book against the heavy water pitcher and started reading as she slowed down her eating, frequently picking up her glass. Delightful!

If one couldn't have one's husband dining with one, she thought muzzily, then surely this had to be considered second-best. The champagne *was* delicious. Reading and eating, she was barely conscious of how often she refilled her glass.

The food was gone and she had not completely emptied the bottle, but there was bread and—oh, how thoughtful, an assortment of cheeses. Happily, Page filled her bread-and-butter plate and poured another glass.

When Rupert entered the sitting room by way of their sleeping cabin not too long afterward, Page was waltzing all around the table, skirts a-whirl, *Emma* in one hand, an empty champagne bottle in the other.

She came to a halt in front of him, waving book and bottle. "Good evening, husband," she greeted him, breathless but unabashed.

"It seems to have been a very good evening for you." Rupert grinned as he carefully removed the bottle from her grasp. Just a slight touch of his hand sent her toppling backward into an armchair, where she sat smiling up at him foolishly.

He rang to have the dinner table and its contents removed while Page continued to hum the waltz to which she had been dancing.

Sitting on the arm of the sofa, when the door closed behind the steward, "You are over your seasickness, I gather?" Rupert asked.

"Never—sea—sick—in—my—life!" The haughty declaration was somewhat diminished by a hiccup between each word.

"Indeed?" drawled Rupert, looking and sounding superior. "You mean it was solely my imagination that I held your head over a basin only yesterday evening?"

"I was upset about our marriage," Page retorted, almost stung into sobriety, "not seasick."

"Indeed?" said Rupert again. "How flattering. A bit soon to be sick of one's husband," he murmured almost to himself.

Page stood, holding out her arms for balance, and sashayed up in front of him.

"I wasn't sick of *you*," she explained earnestly, "just a little—little—little—"

"Little little little what?" her husband asked helpfully.

She glared at him. "Rid-i-cul-ling me no s'lu-sollu—"

"Solution?"

"Right. S'lu-shun. I was un-easy."

Without rising from the arm of the sofa, he reached out and pulled her close to him, keeping a hand on either side of her waist.

"Uneasy about what, Page?"

"Why—I married you."

"I hoped," he said almost diffidently, "that it

might be because, despite our differences, you loved me."

"Vicky loved you. Poor little Vicky—she fell in love with you when she was just seven years old."

"And who," asked Rupert quietly, "is Vicky?"

"Me. I am. The little girl in Cornwall you gave your very first fossil to. Remember? And I gave you a sketch of yourself. Or did you forget that, too?"

"I forgot nothing. The sketch hangs in my bedroom at the Dower House. And the picture of the bone is in my library. As for the fossil, I have it with all the other specimens in the laboratory, waiting till I start my museum."

"*You* have it . . . b-b-but you c-can't. I threw it away. When we quarreled and you misjudged me, I got angry, and I threw it away." She sounded weepy. "I was s-so s-sorry afterward."

Rupert pulled her closer. "Save your tears. My clever little sisters rescued *our* fossil, treasure box and all. It's the truth I'm telling you. I have it in my laboratory at home."

Page gave a few joyful sniffs, then wiped her nose on the back of one sleeve. In one quick motion, Rupert shifted from the arm of the sofa to the sofa itself and brought Page with him, square in the middle of his lap. She snuggled there quite happily.

"Now tell me about misjudging you, little Vicky," he said, with his lips against her hair. "What was between you and my stepmother?"

Page scrambled off his lap and onto the sofa beside him. "I don't like to be called Vicky," she said, sitting very tensely, her voice tightly controlled. "Vicky belonged to someone else. *Page* is Caroline Llanwelly's daughter."

"Very well, Page it shall be . . . in spite of my fond memories of little Vicky."

"Do you remember your stepmother's name before she married your father?"

"She was a Wellington-Ware, I think," Rupert said after a moment's reflection.

"Before she married, she was," said Page. "Her first husband was Harlan Page—my father."

"What!"

Page stood up. She was completely sober now. "Do you remember," she asked, "when you inquired about my passport, I said that it had expired and Marcus arranged a new one for me in the name of Vaile? Well, that was as true as many of the other stories I told you; it hadn't expired. I have it with me. Would you wait a moment, please."

She walked slowly into the sleeping cabin and returned with an open passport, which she held out before him. "This was my legal name before I married you."

He read the name in disbelief. "Diane Victoria Page. Diane is your *mother?*" he asked her incredulously.

"Legally, yes. I assure you, in no other way."

"What happened?"

"Ask Diane," Page shrugged, "not me. I only now that I lived at Cliff House in Cornwall ith Caroline Ettington, later Caroline Llan-elly, from the time I was four years old. I was isited occasionally by my mother; then she arried your father, and there were no visits at ll. She provided money, and later so did Lord aile—for the woman he considered Diane's be-ved old governess."

She gave a hard little laugh. "Pray don't look) distressed. As it turned out, Diane did me a emendous favor. God knows the mother I lost as nothing; the one I gained was everything I uld ever want, and she gave me a wonderful ther and three brothers, too. Nevertheless, I ave despised your stepmother most of my life."

"Good God!" said Rupert fiercely, pulling her ack onto his lap. "Despise her, you only despise er!"

"I don't want your father to know; it would istress him to no purpose."

"That's very generous of you, my love."

Sweetly conscious of that *my love,* even at ich a time, Page shook her head.

"You *could* destroy her, you know," Rupert ointed out.

"I no longer care to," said Page, "and I certain- don't want to destroy *our* sisters."

"Good God!" Rupert said again. "So they are. n different sides of the family, as much your isters as mine!"

They sat for several minutes in silence, both

with a great deal to think over. Presently, R
pert turned her around to face him. "We have
great deal to talk about, but somehow I do
want to do it now. . . . The main barriers stan
ing between us seem to have been torn down. I
you suppose that perhaps we could table oth
matters for a while and consider seriously th
business of being married?"

Page's heart, which had been skipping happi
about inside her chest, took a sharp, straig
dive to the level of her Roman-style slippers.

There was no mistaking the passion in h
voice, the intent behind his set face and th
hands busy at the waist ties of her negligee.

Once again she slid off his lap and sto
facing him.

"There's just one l-little th-thing m-more, R
pert," the new Mrs. Vaile told him with a sick
smile.

Chapter Twenty-eight

THE FULL STORY HAD BEEN TOLD—NOT WITHOUT
few tears and rambling apologies mixed in
with her explanations. Finished at last, Page
stood before her husband, prepared for wrath,
resentment, or shock. She was equally ready to
defend Eliza from his criticism and disgust or
herself from any variety of unpleasant recrimi-
nations.

His reaction was totally unexpected. In the
contemplative way of a scholar or scientist sum-
ming up the results of a body of knowledge,
Rupert said, "Do you know, I'm inclined to agree

with your mother? She is really a woman
quite superior understanding. It's obvious,"
informed her smugly, "that you are madly
love with me and, being too proud to let go
your grudge and acknowledge it, you seized h
of Eliza's predicament to justify your change
heart. Mind you," he finished, extremely se
satisfied, "you were justifying it to yourself, n
to me."

"Why, you—you conceited oaf!" gasped Pag

He ignored that wifely interjection.

"The only thing I wouldn't have believed,"
continued in that same thoughtful way, "is th
you could be such a frightened rabbit."

Page stepped toward him, eyes glitterir
"What do you mean, frightened rabbit?"

"Cowering in your cabin, pretending to ha
seasickness in order to avoid an honest confro
tation with the husband who adores you," R
pert reminded her gently, "was hardly the act
an intrepid woman."

"I wasn't afraid. I was just—just—I didi
know how to tell you."

"And perhaps you weren't in a hurry to
suggested her husband. "After all, avoidan
did delay the—er—lovemaking which mig
have followed afterward."

Fury darkened her eyes to navy blue. "Are y
calling me a coward?"

Rupert rubbed the knuckles of one hand alo
his chin. "I believe," he said cautiously,
might be."

300

Lightning sparks darted out of the now-stormy ue-black eyes. "Are you saying that I'm fright- ed of—of *that*—of *you*?"

Rupert shrugged. "The thought had occurred me," he admitted. "Some virgins are a bit ore afraid than they acknowledge about . . ." e stared at the ceiling for inspiration—"about e exercise of husbandly prerogatives," he fin- hed blandly.

Page tore so savagely at the waist ties of her egligee, one of the velvet bows came off in her nds. She tossed it onto the floor and her ecious negligee followed after it. Then she sat wn on the carpet, untying the crossed cords of r slippers.

"Page, may I—"

She looked up for a second to glower at him. on't you dare speak to me." She pulled off her ippers and threw them in his general direc- n. Through his judicious ducking, one of em missed Rupert's head and landed against e wall; the other went sailing out of the port- le.

"One is no good without the other," said Ru- rt philosophically as he turned to flip the maining slipper through the porthole to join mate in the sea.

When he turned back to her, Page was almost t of her nightgown. He watched, torn between nusement and arousal, as she tugged it over r head, inside out, and then dropped it in an tidy heap at her feet.

"Well," she demanded fiercely, "what are y
standing over there for? Come on, damn y
and exercise those prerogatives I'm supposed
be so afraid of."

She was everything he had dreamed of sin
the day he first saw her standing on the dock .
those beautiful long limbs hinged by a patch
thistledown the same wheat color as the h
streaming down her straight, proud back. S
had the full-breasted, slim-waisted, rour
hipped figure that most women could o
achieve with cruel corseting and unhealthy l
ing.

She was beautiful and magnificent, and s
was openly, avowedly his . . . and he could ha
ly take advantage of the invitation tendered
this marvelous Naked Fury because he was
doubled up with laughter, he could hardly sta
upright, let alone walk across to her.

"Well?" Her bare toes set up an impatie
tapping. "Are you just going to stand there cac
ling all night or are you planning to take me?

"Oh, I'm going to take you, all right,"
finally managed to gasp out, "but just give m
few minutes, please . . . and then, could we p
sibly lie down and, perhaps, do the thing a
more gradually and in comfort?"

"Why consult *me* about technique?" she sn
ped. "*I'm* the inexperienced one, remember?"

"So you are," said Rupert. "So you are."

Suddenly he stopped laughing. They sto

taring at one another, more like antagonists
han lovers; then he swooped down on her,
fting her into his arms and high against his
hest.

Page squirmed a little in mixed excitement
nd dismay as his two hands made contact with
er bare bottom.

"But not for long, my darling," Rupert whis-
ered in her ear. "Not for long."

He carried her into the sleeping cabin, laid her
n her berth, and swiftly began his own undress-
ng. Page lay curled on her side, watching him.
he rest may not have gone according to her
omantic plan, but one thing was going to be as
xpected . . . bare skin against bare skin.

When he was ready to join her, she quietly
iade room for him. They lay side by side, not
ouching, till Rupert put out one hand to smooth
ack her hair. "I'm almost afraid to say, 'Don't
e afraid,'" he whispered lovingly, "but darling,
lease don't be afraid. We'll take it slow and easy
nd . . ."

Page's arms went around him in a strangle-
old. "For pity's sakes," she said. "I'm not afraid
-not anymore—and I'm damned tired of being a
irgin wife."

His laughter rang out again as he gathered her
) him, then eased himself above her. "And I'm
ist as tired of having one," he assured her.

"So let's do something about it."

"We are about to," promised her husband,

bending his head and bringing her close for l
kiss.

After a long breathless moment, their li
parted.

"Aren't you going to put out the lamp?" s
inquired shakily.

"And miss the sight of your naked loveliness
not on your life. You're the one who claims t
body is a thing of beauty to behold."

"Let me look at yours then." Page tried to pu
him back from her.

He resisted, pressing forward onto h
"Afterward," he whispered. "We'll look aft
ward."

But afterward they were much too exhaust
to do anything but lie together, sleepily sat
and utterly if silently satisfied.

Not till after the second go-round did th
have what Page was pleased to call the
exhibit and her husband decided was a pleasa
ly uninhibited exploration of their newly p
sessed selves.

"Do you know," she exclaimed delightedly
one point, her fingers tracing a very persor
path downward from his chest, "I shall make
very much better painter now that I am m
ried?"

"Anything to help the cause of art," said R
pert, one arm stretched over her, one a
stretched under her, and every other muscle
his body supine.

"Darling," said Page presently, having examined his ribs and all the territory south of them, "you're not too upset about Eliza, are you?"

"Eliza," he repeated languidly.

"Eliza." As his eyes showed no enlightenment, she elaborated sarcastically, "You remember Eliza, don't you? Your—I should say, *our* sister."

"Oh, Eliza."

"I know it must seem terrible to you, at her age doing—well, what we just did—but it doesn't mean she's—and we'll have her—and Emily—at the Dower House with us most days, so you don't have to—"

Rupert exerted himself to turn over toward her. "You think," he said in strangely amused tones, his head propped up on one elbow, "that I am troubled about Eliza's virtue?"

"Well, aren't you?"

"Not really." He yawned, and his elbow gave way, his head plopped down again on the pillow. "Seeing as how she's just as much a virgin now as you were one short hour ago."

Suddenly wide awake and alert, Page bounced upright beside him, her bare breasts jiggling against his ribs.

"Say that again."

Obligingly, he repeated his remark.

"She wasn't—she didn't—she never—the drawing master—"

"Is fifty years old, a most respectable ma
with a wife and seven children."

"She made it all up, that whole pathetic story
The letter which brought me into Derbyshir
was—was—"

"Contrived? A fake? Made up?"

"Well, was it?"

"All three, I'm afraid," said her husband wit
no visible sign of regret.

"I shall kill her!" said Page with quiet viciou
venom. "Dear God, I will strangle her with m
bare hands." She clutched at her hair, the
lifted her clenched fists heavenward. "When
think of the anguish she put me through . . .
She pounded her husband's chest. "Bring her t
Italy quickly so I can get my hands on her."

Rupert lay comfortably, watching and lister
ing as she raved on for several minutes, waitin
for the inevitable moment when her eyes na
rowed in suspicion and she looked down at hir
in stark, surprised horror.

"How do *you* know she faked the whole affair
My God, Rupert, *you* didn't plan it, did you, an
make that poor little girl a party to such a—suc
a—"

"Calm yourself, Page, my imagination is no
so fertile. It was all Eliza's scheme, and it took
bit of convincing on her part," he added sel:
righteously, "before *I* consented."

"But you knew—you *knew* all along—you—
you—when I came to you and asked you to marr

306

me, and at the wedding . . . the whole time . . . you *knew*?"

"I knew."

"And all of yesterday when I sat in this blasted cabin . . . starving and alone?"

He nodded his head. "And while we're confessing, I may as well go the whole way. Good old Charley Witherspoon is not on board. Although it's true he married Beasley's daughter, I haven't seen him since our Eton days."

"I'll kill *you*!"

"Why should you?"

"You tricked me, you bastard!"

"Why is that worse than your trying to trick me?"

"What are you talking about?"

Rupert quoted soulfully, "A long honeymoon in Italy because you couldn't live without me . . . and all the while you were planning to palm the real bastard off on me!"

"That was different."

"In what way was it different?"

Page turned her face away and found herself suddenly seized by the shoulders, and shaken with great thoroughness. "How was it different? Answer me, Page."

She might have been revealing some terrible crime. "Because I *do* love you, damn it!" The words seemed to be forced out of her. "And I didn't want to live without you."

Rupert laughed out loud and rained kisses all

over the now-white shoulders that undoubtedl
would carry bruises from his digging-strong fin
gers the next day.

"Not that I didn't know, but it took you lon
enough to say it," he told her exultantly. "Well
Eliza knew it, too. And she and I decided tha
since you would marry me sooner or later—why
not a little push to make you do it sooner?"

He lay back against the pillows, pulling he
along with him.

"I must admit I had some qualms about goin
along with my darling daring sister, but I'n
damn glad now." His eyes twinkled up at her
"Aren't you?"

Page stared down at him, eyes mutinous, lip
stubbornly set.

Rupert fetched up a deep exaggerated sigh
"My darling wife," he drawled, "you have th
choice between having the truth shaken out o
you or acknowledging it voluntarily and bein
rewarded with some wild and wonderful love
making."

As his arms reached up threateningly, Pag
flung hers down and around him. "All right,"
she shouted. "All right." Then, "I'm ever s
damn pleased," she admitted in a softer voice
wriggling amorously on top of him. "Now giv
me my reward."

Rupert lay still, eyes closed.

"You promised," she said accusingly.

"Don't worry. I have never broken a promis

n my life, and I certainly don't intend to start
vith this one."

He turned over and pulled her beneath him,
kissing her at length and with renewed strength.

"I do love a man of honor," said Page a long
ime later.

Tapestry
HISTORICAL ROMANCES

POCKET BOOKS